THE LOST CITY OF BOOKS

Gregory L Norris

<u>Ordering Information:</u>

Quantity sales. Special discounts are available on quantity purchases by **book clubs,** corporations, associations, and others. For details, contact the publisher at director@vanvelzerpress.com.

<u>Cover design by Miblart</u>

Edits & Layout & Publishing via Van Velzer Press
ISBN: 978-1-954253-00-1

Printed in the United States of America

<u>VanVelzerPress.com</u>

DEDICATED TO ALL THE

WRITERS

AND WRITING

THAT EVER CHANGED THE WORLD

Chapter

One

In the Outer Rings, you can get just about anything—contraband medicine, the cheap liquor they brew from illegal root vegetables, flesh. Anything except knowledge, because all of that went up in smoke during the Redactions almost thirty years ago.

On another bleak morning, I went to one of the hopeless apartment buildings in the upper part of the alphabet—Building E— in search of medicine for my father. A fog hung over the world. It was always foggy, always *grey*; no matter the letter, no matter how far from death you were supposed to be. My father and I lived in Building R, which meant I still had time to save him.

As I was approaching I noted movement in the fog and, despite the heavy cloak I wore to disguise myself as a girl, my flesh prickled with a frisson of fear. The wrongness took shape a breathless instant later in the form of a pair of P.F.R. uniforms standing near the front entrance. You didn't often see the charcoal and teal colors of the People's Free Republic this deep in the Outer Rings, their clothes marked by the familiar symbol of circle within ring.

They didn't come here because they didn't need to—this was a land where even the living were already considered dead. Those uniforms belonged to the Inner Rings and the Core of the city where those in power made decisions.

I willed my gaze away and continued down the pitted sidewalk aware of the gallop of my heart and a sense of defeat. My father needed medicine, and I knew no other source for the elixir that could lower his blood sugar and prevent the grey F.O.G. from stealing more of him. The woman who lived in Building E had, according to whispers, experimented with various rare, local flora and found certain combinations that helped.

For the P.F.R. to have dispatched two and possibly more uniforms to the Outer Rings, that meant news had traveled to the Core of Saturn City. And if it had—

My instincts warned me right as I fell beneath a shadow darker than the morning fog's. I halted, froze. Thawing enough, I tipped a look up; a vision from a nightmare blocked my path.

The Redactor stood at least seven feet tall, but in my silent panic, it towered over me as high as one of the few dead trees left near the Alphabet Complex. In quick order I recorded its attire—black suit and shoes, all of its clothes looking quite dusty and old, like faded ink. Its hands were long and pale, the fingers ending in sharp points. And its head…

I'd seen Redactors a few times before, always at a distance. My nausea intensified at the sight of its hairless, elongated face close up, the dark stains around its cyanotic lips, and those holes that used to be eyes and nose. They say the Redactors changed after inhaling all of the knowledge they burned, those billions and billions of books with all the information they contained. All those incinerated words.

One of the original architects of the Redactions now stood before me, blocking my escape.

I sensed what passed for its scrutiny upon me. Those dark stains where eyes used to be had long ago lost the ability to see. No, this Redactor observed me using the surface telepathy they'd acquired after they changed. I felt its invasion, its thoughts attempting to gossip around inside my head, probing, parasitical. I did what my grandmother told me to and emptied my thoughts, instead focusing on the day's moody, slate palette. A grey fog. The next second tolled with the weight of an eternity.

The horror reached into its jacket pocket and produced a version of a monocle. It fixed the device to its right eye. The monocle lit into a ring of fluorescent white. After another tense moment, the Redactor made a sound—what my imagination translated into a dismissive snort. It glided away, its movements creating a papery rustle in the damp morning air. After all, to it I was only a girl. Inferior. Sub-human. A worthless shadow moving through the grey fog.

I choked down a dry swallow and willed my legs back into motion. At my back, somebody screamed—a woman. The medicine woman, no doubt. I tried to block out the peals of her shrieks and mostly succeeded.

Eyes wide, I walked with blinders on through the fog toward Building D. There, I reversed course, looped around, and headed back in the direction of R. At Building N, I passed a body slumped face down on the patch of brown lawn adjacent the sidewalk. Others out on that foggy morning took no special notice of the dead man's body—it was just one more corpse for the undertakers to drag to the fire pits that ran constantly here in Limbo, a land of lost souls.

* * *

We lived on the ground floor—"lived" being a generous description. The three-room apartment was one of ten on that level of a building with ten stories. As I traveled down the dark corridor that stunk of other people's sweat and cooking, I did my best to ignore the invisible weight pressing down from the concrete, tenants, and despair crammed wall to wall above us. R was only eight letters from Z, but we were closer to the end of the alphabet than the beginning. Most of the occupants around and above us were already functionally dead. They just kept breathing in the polluted air of the Outer Rings, oblivious to that fact.

Sobbing reached my ears just as I passed one of the closed doors. Neighbors came and went all the time, and we rarely got to know their names let alone them. My father and I had traveled from Building C in the beginning to L before being relocated to R three years ago. As I reached for the dirty metal doorknob, I again wondered about the bureaucracy at work in Saturn City's Core—the machine that recorded names, births, deaths, and all the slides toward expiration dates that kept residents coming and going here and in a dozen other Outer Ring ghettos.

The sense of malaise sitting heavy in my gut deepened. I never knew what I would find when I opened the door. My father no longer locked it. He was no longer able to.

Why bother, Palermo? I heard him say in my memory in a tired voice many years older than his actual fifty-one seasons.

There wasn't anything of much value to steal in this crypt. Unlike ancient Egyptian tombs, no gold, jewels, or mummified deity-cats filled treasure vaults; only the barest of possessions and necessities were horded here. The corner of the kitchen had a sink and running water, the bathroom a toilet and shower, both operating on limited, rationed use. A tired sofa left behind by the previous tenants occupied the space beneath the front room's only window. That improvised bedroom, my father's, had the best connection to the F.O.G. My father was huddled in a fetal curl atop the sofa, plugged into the cable as usual. At first, I couldn't tell if he was breathing.

I stood rooted to the spot on a patch of grimy linoleum, that floor never truly clean no matter how hard I scrubbed. I realized I was holding my breath and expelled the volcanic air inside my lungs. I approached the sofa.

"Dad," I said. "*Baba?*"

Lawrence Bistany, my father, roused, a kitten's whimper escaping his lips.

I repeated the sacred word for dad in Arabic—"Baba!"—while hugging him, overcome with relief.

He jolted out of the spell, recognized me through wide-open eyes, and reached for the F.O.G. cable, still connected to the port in his skull. He tugged, severing the link, and winced. Then he grabbed hold of me and shook.

"Don't you ever say that out loud again! *Never*, Pal," he admonished.

The tears I'd kept under control following my encounter with the decades-old ghoul outside Building E stung at my eyes. "I'm sorry," I said.

My father tossed the wall cable, softened his grip, and pulled me down for a hug. He held onto me in a way that verged on painful. The sour, unwashed smell of his hair and body filled my next shallow sip of breath.

"You never know who's listening—*who's in that cursed F.O.G. You have to be more careful, Palermo!*"

I nodded.

"Promise me," he said.

I vowed that I would. He released me. I straightened. My father rolled over, retrieved the cable, and reconnected to the mindless grey noise that was slowly killing him.

* * *

I sat on my bed, an old mattress that we were lucky to have, and stared at the patch of empty, builder-beige wall beside the bedroom door.

In the beginning, appeared at the top in bold, black letters.

I mentally crossed them out.

Once upon a time, I wrote with my mind in ink that was purple. More words appeared, some in azure blue, others in rose red. *A girl who was really a young man named Palermo lived with his father in a hopeless prison located in one of the Outer Rings. He grew his hair long and wore the drab grey robes imposed by the P.F.R. on women from an early age so he could become invisible and discover all that was possible to know. He learned about Ancient Egypt and the other planets in the solar system and what the Redactors did when most of those around him died even when they still drew breath into their lungs and surrendered to the grey F.O.G.*

I stood. The mirror above the dresser was cracked. My Lebanese grandmother, Bernadette, told me that happened during the Mother's Day Massacre after I was born. They hid me in the dying woods that day. So goes the story. We all are the owners of our own stories. I've never asked more about the crack in the glass or how it got there.

I lowered the hood and pulled the constraining fabric up over my head. Staring back, cut down the center by the lightning bolt in the dirty glass, was a naked, willowy body capped in long, dark hair and dressed now only in socks. Palermo Bistany easily passed for a young woman beneath the oppressive garb. He would have while disrobed, too, if not for Adam's apple and cock.

I erased the partial story on the bedroom wall with my mental red pen. More words appeared, these in elegant strokes of green calligraphy.

It's a good thing that neighbors no longer ask names or get to know you and that the Redactors have such poor eyesight.

I was always writing stories, even without paper and pen. Without books. Some of those tales stretched beyond the distant limits of the planet Saturn, others the Outer Rings of Saturn City. Any one of them could get me executed at the hands of the same inhuman murderers who dragged the medicine woman out of her apartment in Building E, never to be seen again.

* * *

To understand the world now, you have to know what it was like then, before the Redactions. People were living their lives on the third planet from Sol in a star system located in the galactic region known as Orion's Arm. Take into consideration the millennia of cruelty and intolerance that came before the mass murders and final book burnings that reshaped the old society into the People's Free Republic. A hundred genocides, starting with Cro-Magnon man against Neanderthals preceding Germany, Armenia, Cambodia, Rwanda, Syria, the slaughter of Native Americans in the New World, and other names on maps that no longer exist—the places and the maps. Think—truly *understand*—the scope of bloodshed sanctioned by religions and creeds and governments, all of which labeled one faction superior to another, one god true and all others blasphemous, one skin color worthy over the rest of humanity's beautiful kaleidoscope. All that came before was only the setup for what culminated during the Redactions, when knowledge was lost, and, with it, whatever remained of our collective soul.

Before the book burnings, you could have a difference of opinion, my grandmother told me. You could disagree, debate a problem from different sides, and work on an amicable solution. But some of the most dangerous in positions of power decided that could no longer be tolerated. There was only one course, one acceptable mindset or god, one way. Everything else was dangerous and needed to be obliterated, and so, along with the dissenters, all art, all music, all literature and knowledge was burned up. The Redactions continued for years, she told me. Enough that the fires darkened the skies and the ashes of Shakespeare, Hawthorne, Mary Shelley, the Brothers Grimm, and the Sisters Dent can still be seen on certain nights, staining the sunset at dusk.

* * *

I trembled, my throat uncomfortably dry, my skin broken in clammy sweat. The weight of the many apartments and living ghosts over our heads again pressed down, making breathing nearly impossible. My teeth chattered despite the unpleasant warmth in the room. I retrieved my disguise from the floor and dressed. Stories wrote themselves across the blank patch of wall.

Today I went to the medicine woman's place, hoping to barter for something to help my father, who is growing greyer by the hour…

"*Palermo,*" called a familiar woman's voice.

I blinked. The wall erased itself.

"Grandma?" I whispered.

"Say it in the old language, like I taught you," she said in that commanding but warm voice I so loved and needed.

"*Situ,*" I said. The word rolled off my tongue, sweet and pure. Of all the words in all the languages suppressed or lost or spoken of in shadowy corners, "Situ" to me was the most sacred. I turned toward the broken mirror. Reflected in the glass was a short yet regal woman with dark hair, olive skin, and a beauty mark wearing a tasteful day dress, a necklace of red beads, and a lady's watch.

My misery evaporated. I smiled.

"Your father?" my situ, Bernadette Bistany, asked.

My voice hitched as I attempted to answer. "Worse, Situ. I tried to get him medicine, but the Redactors and soldiers from the P.F.R. were there."

Sadness washed over her expression. "He needs to get off that sofa, disconnect from the F.O.G. and move around. He needs to *hope* if he's going to survive."

"I know."

"You must make him, Palermo. He's the *baba* and you're the *walad*, but now you must become the baba. Be the bigger man. Save him from the greyness before he withers."

The tears were back. "I missed you."

My situ blurred in the mirror. "I know."

A sense of hopelessness I normally kept ahead of caught up and crashed over me. I collapsed onto the bed, hiding my face behind my hands. Movement stirred before me. The breeze took my wrists and gently lowered them, and my Lebanese grandmother, who perished on that same day of tears as an untold number of mothers and beacons of wisdom and kindness stood in front of me.

"You are unique, Palermo," she said. She cupped the sides of my face and caressed the patch of skull where every other person alive was marked by the F.O.G. connection terminal. "*Special.*"

"Tell me another story, Situ," I implored.

She eyed me, her expression grim around the edges. "One more story?"

"Please."

Her gaze darted from side-to-side, as though to confirm we were truly alone. "Okay, my sweet Palermo. I will tell you the most fabulous of stories. This one is the greatest of mysteries, the most powerful of the world's secrets, and it is completely real."

"The library?" I asked.

Her smile vanished. She nodded.

First

Interlude

This story begins long ago in a distant, lost land located on the eastern littoral of the Mediterranean Sea. The setting is the cedar-lined coast of Lebanon. There, a young girl waits to board a boat that will ferry her from war and bloodthirsty invaders from the east who threaten most of Lebanon's Maronite Catholic population. The young girl's name is Mary.

Mary is alone now. Father left first on a different boat to pass through Ellis Island into the land of opportunities. He traveled ahead to set up a place for the family, to work and earn money he would then use to send for the rest of the small family, one at a time. There's an uncle already there, a tall, ugly man with a big hooked nose who understands how the system works. He's family, so you'd never suspect him of taking poor father's money and not following through with the deal. After all, we're talking a humanitarian crisis! Of course the Nose will do what's right.

And, at first, he does. Mother arrives on the boat from Lebanon following an arduous and perilous journey that is surely a distance of light years and not miles; from one end of the galaxy to the other. Mother disembarks the boat pale and sickly. She rests in the airless heat of the city walkup apartment, almost too ill to move and paralyzed with worry for Mary, her daughter, still at the far end of the universe, and this new land, which is as terrifying in its unfamiliarity as the war-torn Lebanon they've left behind.

The mother recuperates. The father labors, making pitiful wages at backbreaking work to raise enough money to send for Mary.

"This time it costs more," the Nose says.

"Why?" the father asks.

The Nose shrugs. "That's just the way of these things."

The father works even harder. He pays the Nose, his flesh and blood, his kinsman, and trusts that the Nose will follow through on his end of the deal. Even ignoring the money, he's family, so he must be right.

At long last, the full fee is paid, and the Nose, who knows how such matters work, promises that Mary will board the boat, travel across the galaxy, and join the small family of immigrants in this new, safe place that is their home far from the cedar-lined shores of Lebanon.

The mother, still mostly obliterated, picks herself up and struggles down the walkup's stairs and all the way to the pier. She waits, a pale, frail woman with a harsh expression. The boat pulls up to the harbor and docks. Refugees stream out. The mother waits, barely able to draw breath. But Mary isn't among them.

"Maybe tomorrow. Or the next boat after that," the Nose says.

And so, ignoring the misery in her gut, the mother returns the next day, and the following day, barely able to contain her panic when passengers offload. Mary is not among them, never there for the entire year the family remains locked in the same heartbreaking holding pattern before relocating north to a place called Massachusetts.

"I paid for her travel," the Nose maintains. "I don't know what happened."

They believe him—he's family. Only years after the fact does their granddaughter Bernadette, who is born in this new land, question the possibility that the Nose never made the arrangement and instead pocketed the money.

Chapter Two

I sat frozen on the bed, not out of fear but wonder. Blinking myself out of the trance, I wondered how long I'd remained in the same position, transfixed by what my grandmother told me. My body ached, seeming to telegraph more than mere minutes had passed by. I rolled my eyes toward the canvas of beige wall. A million-quadrillion words in every language had been written there but were fading out in the shutter-clicks between blinks. I jumped up and reached toward them, intending to scoop the ink into my hands. But those passages had been written in ectoplasm. Soon, they were gone.

So, too, was the ghost of my grandmother. I performed a turn. Only the room with its sad details greeted my vision.

I sucked down a cleansing breath. The words were gone except in my memory.

* * *

I entered the front room. My father sat up on the sofa but was still connected to the F.O.G. The air smelled sour from his sweat and something my imagination labeled as surrender. His eyes stared out at our small, suffocating world as the darkness beyond the window deepened. But I doubted he saw anything.

"Dad," I said. When he didn't respond, I barked the lone word louder.

He returned enough to locate me among the mindless noise droning in his grey matter. "Pal?"

"Are you hungry?"

He didn't respond.

"Why don't you unplug, take a bath. I'll fix you something to eat."

Long seconds later, he nodded. Reaching up, he worked the F.O.G. cable out of his tangles and attempted to stand on his own. I hurried over to his side and wrapped an arm around his back.

"Can you walk?"

"I can walk," he grumbled, the anger not directed at me—I was merely the closest recipient.

We stood. My father steadied on his feet. I walked him toward the bathroom and only released him when it was clear he could carry forward on his own. As he passed, I caught the rank odor of his urine and found the bedclothes on the sofa damp.

The emptiness inside me attempted to widen. I fought back, filled the void with words, with stories, with truths:

"The names of the planets are, in order, Mercury, Venus, Earth, Mars, Jupiter, ringed Saturn, Uranus, Neptune, and Pluto," I said aloud. "Though, technically, Pluto is a dwarf planet, but it's out there orbiting Sol and I invoke its name when most of the people around me aren't even aware that it exists!"

I stripped the soiled sheets, located the tattered other set that had survived our moves throughout the Alphabet Complex, and remade the sofa into my father's bed. My gaze settled on the F.O.G. cable. As the sound of the shower spilled at my back, I reached toward the wall unit—home of the retracting cable. My rage ignited, my revulsion building to the point I tasted bile.

Like the vanishing words on the bedroom wall, I caught myself about to grab the F.O.G. plug. As my fingertips neared it, the expected, unpleasant slither of energy crackled over my flesh. I'd gone near the units before. It was understandable, even if I didn't possess the data port required to plug into the system.

The Mother's Day Massacre, my inner voice reminded. *Your freedom paid for in the blood of innocents.*

I willed my hand away from the wall unit. It resisted. For the next moment, I didn't so much hear the grey F.O.G. as sense it circling around within the mechanism, the curse of the Redactors and the People's Free Republican dictatorship those monsters had made possible. They describe the F.O.G. as a nothingness, a kind of white noise meant to distract and soothe away cares. Not for the first time, my reaction was different. The nothing projected out of the wall by the Fulfillment Obligation Gadget felt *hungry.*

It was feasting on my father's life and soul. It was giving nothing. It was mesmerizing its prey.

I pulled away and shook out my fingers, thinking they'd been burned by their closeness. The urge to grab some heavy object and pound the F.O.G. connection off the wall nearly overwhelmed me. But to do that would ruin the little we had. My father would be imprisoned and executed for such an act. I'd be unmasked as male, and more alarming to them, also as free of the scalp implant, and all the many stories I contained inside my mind would be lost.

* * *

I opened the foil package. The loaf of M.e.A.L. bore uneven knife marks from the last chunk I'd sliced off to serve us. I caught the smell of the shelf-stable dietary needs product and knew that any bite unlikely enough to make it past my lips would soon reappear on a surge of vomit.

I heated the M.e.A.L. in a pan. They always said Meat-enriched Appetite Loaf tasted better cooked, though some diners swore by it refrigerated. I studied the sear, the green sprinkles in its grey texture that were supposed to be vegetable-based, and suffered a foul hiccup.

To distract myself from my rising nausea, I did another of those brain tests my grandmother was always urging me to perform.

"The names of the nine Muses of Greek mythology are: Erato, Euterpe, Calliope, Clio, Polyhymnia, Terpsichore, Thalia, Melpomene, and Urania."

I switched off the burner and ran water in the sink. Splashing some on my face helped. Not so much when I placed the plate before my father, who chewed in a daze, not seeing and, mercifully, not tasting the meal presented.

Another long night no different from the thousand before it settled over us. I put my father to bed and crawled into mine, aware of the crushing weight of Building R, of life, of the world.

The planet Earth turned in its orbit, and when I woke, the P.F.R. was still in charge and a grey fog hung like a shroud both outside the walls and inside.

* * *

The idea came to me in the night like other dreams before it. If the medicine woman was gone, I'd follow her techniques. I didn't know what plants would specifically benefit my father's condition, but introducing fresh greens and other flora sourced in the wild might improve his health. I didn't think there'd be much in the way of actual danger—P.F.R. soldiers stuck mostly to Saturn's Core and Inner

Rings. I doubted I'd encounter a Redactor out there. Once in two days was enough.

Once in a *lifetime* would have been more than enough.

As for our fellow Alphabet-condemned, few made it a point to travel very far from their F.O.G. connection

So while my father slept, I sneaked out of the building and across the brittle remains of the lawn. I risked a look up. The nearest of the Alphabet buildings braced the overcast morning sky. The sun floated just above the horizon in the east, a platinum disk that only looked half there behind the clouds.

The air thrummed with an undercurrent born of the power systems feeding into the rows of buildings. A familiar raw sewage smell hung in the air. I drew my cowl around my head after scoping out my course. If anyone was out and watching, it wouldn't aid my cause to be seen taking in my surroundings. No one was. This was not a world that welcomed visitors. Women and girls walked with their heads down, a show of obedience, so I again hid my face and advanced.

I hastened around to the back of the buildings, already knowing what I would find there: the old service road. I'd guessed it was used to cart in the supplies to construct the apartments decades earlier. Now, it was a road that led to nowhere other than the fire pits. I continued down the fractured asphalt, past a makeshift basketball court and several broken picnic tables, all that remained of expired youths, ghosts of our past. The edge of the dead forest rose up. None of the nearest trees had put forth new leaves since before we arrived to Building R.

I continued down the old access road, imagining myself as a specter dressed in grey wandering a foggy heath. No birds sang. I tried to remember the last time I'd seen a bird other than a carrion feeder helping itself to some new corpse slumped on the ground between apartments.

The dead trees thickened around me, and the unnerving quiet deepened. I stopped my march and turned. The dead forest surrounded the road. The apartment complex could barely be seen now, towering sepia monsters standing indistinct in the fog.

A shiver teased the nape of my sweaty neck. I fought it, I failed. The chill tumbled down my backbone and sent the world out of focus. When things stabilized, my gaze drifted to the trees of the dead forest. The emptiness inside me widened.

Books.

At one time, books filled with glorious words had been printed upon paper made from wood pulp. The books were gone. So, too, the trees. As I stood there shaking, I couldn't help but think we'd reached the end of time. The world was dead and only going through the final motions set in place by those who'd murdered it. Soon it would all turn to ash. Everything.

As though to confirm this belief, the wind lifted and a foul ribbon of air invaded my nostrils. It was worse than the raw sewer smell always there closer to the Alphabet Complex. Sinking deeper into the malaise that had caught up to me, I realized what I was near.

I moved with stealth. Best not to be seen even by the undertakers. From my vantage behind a dead tree's trunk, I watched the men who operated the body carts unload corpses stacked four and five deep atop the flatbed. There were no elaborate burial customs, no prayers for the dead anymore, and no ceremonial robes on the deceased. One at a time, men offloaded them from the flatbed and dropped them into the fire pit.

The pit, from what I could see, was a gouge carved out of the ground and running in a jagged line far across the lifeless plain. The edge of the fire pit looked to have been plowed over. The dirt bore tracks from heavy earth moving machinery which sat parked alongside some other construction vehicles. I gathered from these clues that when the cremains grew too high in the ravine, the undertakers simply buried over them, and the burning of bodies continued in the newer sections of trench.

They burned bodies with the same lack of regard as the Redactors had once burned books.

Sickened, my gaze lingered. Through the orange tongues of flame and oily black smoke, I could see the remains of skulls and bones, tossed without respect, lives and identities forgotten, gone forever. The undertakers lugged more dead weight down from the flatbed. A body's head, lolling just above the dirt, turned in my direction and, for a terrible moment, the face was my father's. I blinked, and it wasn't. They pitched the corpse into the fire. I turned and vomited everything that wasn't in my stomach behind the trunk of the dead tree.

* * *

An untold distance away, the landscape altered. Green blades and leaves appeared, a few at first but more proof that the world hadn't fully expired.

I came upon a copse of trees, all living, and my hope surged. A ridge of what I at first mistook for boulders rose ahead of me. Vines and sedge covered the rocks. Nearing, I realized the ridge was really the bombed-out remains of a concrete building. A warm, green fragrance infused the air. I wandered around the ridge to find myself staring at a view that stole my breath.

A valley spread before me, damp and green beneath the thinning overcast. Actual blue sky appeared through breaks in the clouds. The green wasn't merely green but colored in spots by yellows, reds, and purples. All of this vibrancy had been superimposed over the remains of a dead city. Through the encroaching canopy, I made out the skeletons of buildings, metal spires, and bridges.

How long have I walked?

I forced my eyes away from the fallen city down to my feet. My old shoes looked far older and were caked in dirt. At that moment, the ache in my legs and lower spine caught up to my awakening senses, filling my muscles with fire. I had walked to the end of the planet, I was sure. For a shocking second, I wondered if this was Lebanon.

Then I turned. Visible at the limit of the horizon was the uppermost floor of one of the Alphabet apartments. I'd traveled far past the Outer Rings and the burial pits but was still just within sight of all that was familiar and wrong. From somewhere nearby, a bird squawked. I wouldn't say its song was pretty, but in that instant it was the most beautiful sound I could recall. I unstuck and wandered forward down a grassy knoll and closer to the fallen city. This was a place from before the Redactions; it was part of a civilization that had been destroyed.

Another sound rose up from the wild tangles that surrounded me. At first, I confused the thrum with that of the grey F.O.G. Only this didn't crawl across my flesh or nauseate me. No, it was the lazy chirrup of insects living in the green. I smiled and even risked a laugh.

There would be healthy, pure nutrition here among the wilderness steadily reclaiming the fallen city. I wasn't entirely sure where to look or even which plants were safe, but I intended to find them, even if it required trial and error.

I leaned down, not wanting to pick the crimson blossom, only smell its fragrance. I waited patiently while a fuzzy, buzzing yellow and black pollinating insect danced over its petals collecting nectar, aware of the wide smile on my face. When the pollinator flitted on, I indulged. My lungs filled with an otherworldly sweetness. I gasped and breathed more in quick, desperate sips until I grew lightheaded in an attempt to clean my body of the toxic world at my back.

Not far from the flowers, I came upon another tangle of thorny brambles. These were covered in a kind of blue-black berry that also exuded a sweet fragrance. I couldn't tell if the fruit was safe other than by the fact that many of the cones were empty, those berries plucked clean. Since I didn't find any animal or bird carcasses around the bushes, I judged them safe and removed one from the brambles. A tart, delicious taste exploded on my tongue. I ate a dozen more, breaking my own new rule about waiting to see if anything I ate here was toxic. I'd downed another twenty before I stopped myself and rationalized the proper steps I should be taking.

Those berries… I swore I could taste the sun's light on them. They sat in the emptiness of my gut, refreshing and wholesome. I opened the bag I'd brought and gathered more, stopping every dozen or so to indulge in another taste. Purple juice coated my fingers.

I followed the brambles around a stone obelisk then further along a courtyard of fractured concrete, in my excitement letting down my guard, which was never wise. I knew better. As though to remind me of the danger, I noted that the happy chirrup of insects had evaporated. A chill settled over my flesh despite my sweat. The silence broke in a papery slither, a sound of dead leaves stirring in a cold breeze.

Holding my breath, I turned.

Standing near the obelisk was a Redactor, the one who wore a monocle, and its enlarged black eye hole was aimed in my direction.

Second Interlude

The young girl skipped along the pitted sidewalk, mindful of the cracks but believing them no real threat to her progress. After all, with very little effort, she imagined herself gliding over the breaks. Yes, she'd spread her arms and catch the afternoon air, even though no breeze blew and the heat sat on top of the city, oppressive and merciless.

Her grandparents' apartment house appeared, a triple-decker two up from the weedy banks of the Spigot River. The familiar mix of excitement and anxiety in equal doses filled her, helped along by the musty smell of the river and that of mowed grass. The thin strip of front yard behind the chain link fence had been buzzed, the remains of the blades left to bake and crinkle atop the lawn.

The girl unhooked a metal latch and pushed through the gate. She remembered to close it before her mother's voice nagged into her thoughts. From there, she skipped along the distance past the first-floor windows where the younger couple lived—they were still a million times older than she and had twin baby girls—and to the main entrance, which was housed under a gabled portico. She thumbed the middle buzzer and looked up at the curtained living room window. After a while, a face appeared; round, *sad*.

"*Situ, it's me,*" she called. "Bernadette."

The door buzzed. The girl pushed through, remembering the many times she'd waited one second too late to enter only to discover that her grandmother was gone from the window, the door still locked, leaving her to start the entire process all over again.

Bernadette skipped through into the hallway. The door to the downstairs apartment stood open. Bernadette expected the mom to rush out and scold her for making too much noise, for waking the twins, or any of the other ludicrous crimes she was always being accused of committing. But Bernadette had recently decided she wasn't guilty and the self-appointed judge, jury, and executioner that lived beneath her grandparents no longer held any authority over her.

The staircase had bottled a ghost of perfume and the reassuring trace of allspice from her situ's cooking. The heat followed her inside and sat thick at the top of the second-floor landing. Bernadette cast a look at where the stairs continued up to the third-floor apartment and was grateful her journey went only as far as here.

Bernadette waited outside the door. She caught the shuffle of her grandmother's steps across the crackled linoleum of the kitchen floor, their gait heavy, slow, and, the girl imagined, burdened with pain. The door opened. The air barely stirred. Bernadette's grandmother stood in the stagnancy, clad in an old housedress and slippers. Bernadette's worry surged. Her grandmother barely smiled on the best of days, but on this scorcher it was as though a ghost had answered her knock.

Still, calling upon her inner optimist, the girl bounded over and embraced her grandmother, ignoring the heat radiating off the ghost's body and the bitter tang of her sweat.

"Granddaughter," Situ said. "Why are you here?"

Bernadette broke the hug and closed the door. All of the windows in the apartment were opened, but none of the fans were on. Not asking for permission—and knowing she wouldn't get it—

Bernadette switched on the one sitting dormant on her grandmother's oval kitchen table. The relief was instant and welcome.

"Your mother send you over to check up on me again?" Situ asked.

"Yes. *No*," Bernadette answered. "I'm here to spend time with you. Help out. Keep you company." She eyed the dishes in the sink, more than a day's worth, Bernadette guessed. "Where's Grandpa?"

"Your *jiddo* is out working," Situ said on the slow amble back to an overstuffed chair in the living room.

Bernadette absorbed that bit of intelligence with a scowl kept mostly hidden. *Working* meant he was up to no good—gambling, lollygagging, or worse. "Good," she said. "Because I'm here for *you*, Situ."

Her grandmother waved a hand in dismissal as she sat. Bernadette entered the living room. The fan in there, set atop the record player's exquisite rosewood cabinet, wasn't moving. Jiddo didn't let her grandmother listen to her favorite music for the same reason as the inert fans—the cost of electricity.

"It's got to be about a billion degrees in here," the girl said.

She snapped on this fan. Its metal blades spun, circulating the air and driving out most of the misery. Her grandmother moaned, the barest smile cracking her sad expression. The lightness was there one instant, gone the next.

"No, switch off fan," Situ said in her broken English. "Electric bill!"

"Frig the electric bill," Bernadette said. "I'll get you a cool drink."

She found lemonade in the fridge, didn't care if it was Jiddo's, and poured a tall glass with ice for her grandmother. Bernadette handed it over. "You drink this, Situ. I'll tidy up and then we can play cards."

A game of Solitaire was stalled on the kitchen table, how long it had sat there waiting for its sole participant to return Bernadette didn't know. She swept the floor and did the dishes. While gathering up the cards for games that required two players, she heard her grandmother crying in the other room.

The cheery mask dropped from the girl's face. She set down the cards and hastened to her grandmother.

"*Mary*," Situ sobbed.

Chapter Three

Fear gripped me.

The Redactor was dressed similarly to the others I'd encountered from afar—a threadbare black suit over a dirty white button-down, thin black tie, and scuffed shoes. In the radiance of the sunlight, its presentation was even more rumpled and dingy than before. It looked like a thing made of dust; a piece of hate only half there, frail and ready to blow apart on the next breeze. Yet I knew its appearance as a weak thing was deceptive. All I had to do to remind myself of the mortal danger I now found myself in was to recall years of book burnings and murders that had, in effect, destroyed the world.

My only advantage was the sunlight. Redactors didn't see well in any light. Bright light could make it functionally blind—its telepathy required it to focus and concentrate in order to detect its prey. It pivoted away from me, alerted to something elsewhere in the nearby landscape of the fallen city, which was enough for me to thaw and act. I slipped as quietly as possible toward the only cover available—the blackberry brambles—and suffered the scrape of the thorns across my arms and cheeks.

The Redactor turned back and reached up, activating its monocle. The device lit, becoming what I guessed was a sort of heads-up display meant to enhance what was left of its physical vision. If it faced me directly, brambles alone wouldn't provide adequate cover.

I receded farther, coming to a concrete wall. The thorns were pressed up close to the impediment, but I noticed a fracture perhaps a yard away, one that led into darkness beyond its threshold. I studied the Redactor the best I could through the cover of leaves, thorns, and berries. When it looked away, its monocled eye taking in the rest of the courtyard, I slipped toward the break in the wall. My disguise snagged on thorns. I attempted to free the cloak without giving away my location. More thorns punctured my arm. I suffered the stings in silence reaching the opening, ducking into the cool shadows *mostly* unnoticed.

The Redactor slithered nearer. I peered around the concrete. A fluorescent beam of light strafed the brambles and reached past the fenestration, projected from the Redactor's monocle. Holding my breath, I waited; the cool, dank air settling across my sweating and bleeding flesh. The beam cut out. The Redactor moved on.

What is it doing here? Only after I remembered how to breathe did I make the connection—the medicine woman. If they'd tortured her, she'd have told them about this place. This was where she'd gone to source her flora from the new meadows and forests sprouted over the remains of the fallen city.

I waited. A rumble shook the sky, proof of P.F.R. transport ships. Then the punch of an explosion hammered the fallen city. I caught the flash even in my hiding place. Another followed, close enough that the detonation shook the dark ceiling over my head and pelted me with flecks of cement.

They were bombing the fallen city!

No, it's not the city—the GREEN! my inner voice corrected.

Incinerate the healthy food source before anyone else in the Outer Rings learns of its location and benefits. Scorch everything good—a familiar Redactor tactic.

Orange light flashed past the threshold. I caught the foul smell of accelerant on the wave of the concussion. Oily black smoke billowed out there, noxious with the toxic odor of a defoliant. My way blocked, I started to panic. Then a frigid calm washed over me. I turned, the way behind me dark, indistinct, and uncertain. But it was the only hope of escape, and so I took it.

It never occurred to me that there might be animals or worse in that abyss. Not until I was feeling my way through the darkness, traveling in my thoughts to the very center of the Earth just like in the lost classic by a writer named Jules Verne.

* * *

My eyes adjusted enough that I figured I'd come upon a cellar that connected to another in a network that traveled in a mostly straight line. Twice the corridor turned left. Once, I was forced to wade through standing water that reeked of swampland and rose up to my knees, fueling my anxiety. But I made it past, only to reach a wall of solid cinderblocks, the end. My next breath proved almost impossible, the air around me putrid and clotted.

"No, no, no," I stammered.

I turned around. There, again to my left, I'd missed something. Right after the underground swamp, a break formed in the cinderblock wall, a potential way out!

Dirt and rocks had spilled down, nearly covering the passage's opening. I sucked in a breath and hurried over, thinking but not certain that I detected a faint stir of air and that the darkness had lightened beyond the gap. I pushed. More dirt slid around me, and my mind went to another classic tale lost because of the Redactors, this one about a premature burial. It was possible that a ton of earth was about to slam down upon my head.

It didn't.

I dug my way through the cellar wall and into another basement lined in cement. This one was the end of the network. Oblong windows covered over with chicken wire looked out on overgrown weeds, but enough light filtered through to illuminate my new surroundings. The basement contained a few sticks of furniture and a weight bench. A wooden staircase soared up to the remains of a door standing ajar.

"A house?" I wondered aloud, my voice sounding like it had been shouted in the oppressive silence.

The only ways out of the cellar were either through one of the prison windows or up that staircase. If the latter was as old as I worried—three decades since the Redactions started, plus however long before—I didn't trust it to be safe. But I had no real alternative. I set my hand on the rail and took my first step up. The ancient wood complained with an arthritic creak. I ascended past second and third steps. My foot cracked through the brittle fourth, but I recovered. I counted seventeen in all and reached the door at the top of the stairs.

The door refused to budge, the floor beneath was warped. I pushed harder. The door splintered off its hinges, and I stepped into the remains of a hallway. To one side was another shattered door leading into what I assumed was a ground-floor apartment. What little I made out was in shambles. At the other end, another staircase led to the upstairs. The varnished dark wood walls were pitted with what could only be bullet holes, a scene of past brutality.

The other door before me led to a portico front entrance. I worked the door open and stepped outside. The nearest house was gone apart from its foundation and the cinders left behind by a few walls, proof of a conflagration that had happened long ago. I listened for more detonations. The eerie quiet continued around the house.

The bombing raids were, I gathered, over for now. The greenest area, the sweet valley, was gone.

I turned to face the house. The sad hulk of a three-story box brooded against a sky stained in billows of black smoke. Something about the place looked familiar, though I'd never been there before reaching the end of the underground tunnel network.

Triple-decker, said the voice in my head.

I knew this house!

Through my grandmother.

I navigated past the burned shell and foundation, along a rusted fence, and found myself staring down at the muddy bottom of a river—though *former* river was more of an appropriate description. Maybe it was an actual river when it rained. The depression led me to think the Spigot had been drained or diverted by the same architects who'd bombed the green to prevent the doomed population in the Outer Rings from accessing food or water that wasn't controlled by their authority.

I wandered a ways, following the Spigot's former course in the direction that would take me back to the Alphabet Complex. Twice, the roar of troop transports sent me running for cover. I peered out in time to catch a glint of metal in the smoky sky racing away, headed in the direction of the Inner Rings and Core of the P.F.R. stronghold. Whatever destruction they'd waged was done for now.

Checking the bag strapped to my shoulder, I found the berries still mostly whole and exuding the fresh, pure sweetness of healthy food. My baba was all alone in our hopeless prison, likely plugged into the grey F.O.G. and with no idea that I was gone. A sudden urgency to reach him possessed me. I cut across an overgrown courtyard and through another neighborhood of abandoned houses. Beneath a bridge that still stood, and then the bitter char of the burning green struck me. Smoke rolled in dense clouds carried along by the wind. I covered my nose and mouth with my hand and forged forward. It was the only way back to my father.

* * *

The smoke and the fire.

The smoke.

And the fire.

I tried to imagine what it was like back then, during the Redactions. Electromagnetic pulses had wiped clean the majority of knowledge stored on disks and devices. But, according to the stories my grandmother had shared, the physical knowledge—the books—had been stacked as high as mountain ranges and set ablaze. All of the words and truths paid for over the centuries in blood, all of the stories dreamed and fantastic worlds explored on the page, got burned up along with history. You could see it from space via those electronic eyes still up there in orbit at the time. The books burned on for years, and the Redactors who lit the flames were altered; their bodies no longer human after absorbing the ashes of our cursed race.

The green belt I'd come upon earlier in the day was gone, set on fire. The fallen city's outskirts crackled. I plodded across the scorched earth, my steps kicking up smoke and cinders.

* * *

The complex towered above the dead forest, the light from its uppermost floors looking sallow against the night. Above us, a thousand stars swam in the breaks between clouds. The greatest of dreamers had visited them—Asimov, Le Guin, Dick, Serling, and Bradbury. But their adventures were gone now and nobody traveled far past Saturn anymore.

In the dark, I stumbled over unfamiliar ground in search of the access road. I realized I'd come out of the fire pit area closer to the end of the Alphabet. Closer to death. Buildings T and U. Once you hit O, you were pretty much running out of tomorrows anyway.

I located the road. Exhaustion threatened to overwhelm me. I had walked to the end of the known world and survived another encounter with a Redactor in a destroyed land and welcomed my return to even our miserable room and its bed, where I knew I would sleep.

I plodded up to the rear of the building and sensed unwanted eyes upon me. Several men sat atop the old tables near the basketball court. If they were from this point in the alphabet, chances were solid they were Foggy, not much of a threat. Unless they were like me, the children of parents succumbing to the grey F.O.G., doomed to become orphans. I didn't know our neighbors but assumed the men on the tables out in search of fresher air than what was found in the Alphabet buildings were young, bored, and angry.

I was dressed like a woman. Fresh panic bloomed in my gut, making me walk faster. Something lewd got uttered at my back. I rounded the building and walked through the busted security door, not feeling any less relieved to be back.

* * *

The hallway had jealously bottled its usual repellant smells—that fetor of despair and ghosts. I did my best to walk with invisible blinders on, as I normally did. But my brief encounter with future orphans had left my eyes wide open, and so I saw.

Saw the door to an apartment across the hall was opened.

The apartment was laid out in a mirror reflection of ours. A body was slumped on the floor, not moving. It was still connected to the wall cable for the F.O.G. I searched for any sign of movement. The neighbor's chest didn't rise or fall. *Dead*, I knew.

I froze and kept looking. Almost as terrible to see was the other body, this one seated at an awkward angle on a dirty armchair. That body still breathed, though the rises and falls of its chest were shallow. By the garb, I assumed she was the dead man's wife. She, too, was plugged into the grey F.O.G., one more corpse that hadn't yet fully expired.

I remembered my baba and forced myself to continue on to our apartment. A few steps shy of the door, my worry re-ignited. It was always the same, because I didn't know what I would find when I entered. And I'd been gone for most of the day.

The sofa was empty. The door closed behind me, and the sour weight of the air pressed down.

"*Ba—?*" I started, only to catch myself. "Dad?"

He didn't answer.

I unslung my bag of life-giving, purple fruit and set it on the counter. The apartment wasn't big enough to contain hiding places. I checked my room first, worried he was outside in the night, searching for me. Worse, already gone and being consumed by the fires that devoured every good thing in this world.

As that thought crossed my mind, I spied him on the bathroom floor.

"*Baba!*" I exclaimed, not caring who heard my invoking of forbidden words from many of the lost tongues of the former people of the Earth.

My father grunted something as I helped him to sit up. His eyes attempted to focus on me but instead stared through into a different world. "Pal?"

"Here, Dad," I said.

In quick order, I deduced what had happened—the foul smell of urine from the floor and him, his confusion. I had left. He'd disconnected from the F.O.G. and, while doing his best to relieve himself, had lost his balance and spilled across the bathroom floor.

"I'm here, Dad," I repeated, resting my cheek against his and cradling his head.

"Where did you go?"

To the lost city of Atlantis, I thought. *To the Black Forest of the Brothers Grimm. And around the world in a hot air balloon ride with Jules Verne.*

"For provisions," I settled for instead.

I kissed the sweaty side of his face.

"Let's get you off the floor and cleaned up," I said.

I was bedraggled and sore, but not so destroyed that I couldn't do for my father all I promised.

Once the clean up was finished, I sat him on the sofa and presented him with a bowl filled with berries.

"Eat these," I encouraged.

My father eyed the purple berries with suspicion. "What are they?"

"Surely, you must remember."

He blinked. "Blackberries?"

"Food—real food that contains the warmth of the sun."

With that, he came farther out of the fog. "Pal, where did you find these?"

"Does it matter?"

"Yes—this food is illegal!"

"Then eat the evidence quickly before anyone finds out," I said in a fatherly tone, as my grandmother had urged.

My father stopped arguing. He ate a handful of the berries. His expression instantly brightened. I watched him roll the food across his tongue, tasting it in a way he never would have the putrid M.e.A.L. that he subsisted on.

"Great, aren't they?" I asked.

He grunted in response and swallowed. I waited to see if he'd keep the berries down.

"More," he said.

"Okay, okay," I laughed while adding another heaping handful from the bag to his bowl.

My father ate. He washed the meal down with water from the tap.

"You're a good son," he said.

"I'm trying to be," I said. "Because I have a good dad."

I waited for him to say more. When he didn't, I kissed his forehead, had him stretch out on the sofa, and pulled the sheet up to his neck.

"Goodnight, Baba," I whispered.

I returned to my room, hopeful that I'd shepherded my father back from the abyss. Sleep claimed me the moment I closed my eyes.

When I woke up, I discovered him back in the same fetal curl and plugged into the device that was killing him.

Third
Interlude

They lost track of the time playing games of Whist and Go Fish, which Bernadette's situ pronounced as Go *Vish* when prompted for 2s, 8s, or Queens.

With the fans running, they didn't hear the clomp of footsteps across the driveway or up the stairs, only the grumble of voices when the two men entered the kitchen, and by then it was too late.

"What is this?" her grandfather demanded in his slightly nasal voice, which Bernadette always found sharp on the ear.

Eliosh, her jiddo, snapped off the fan in the kitchen and hurried into the living room to do the same. Her grandmother was winning the latest game, probably not suspecting that Bernadette had allowed her to, but the match, at that second, effectively ended. Jiddo wasn't a big man, and Bernadette thought his mustache ridiculous, the way it continued down the sides of his face to end in two sharp points, the rest sitting thick like a caterpillar on his upper lip. But he could sometimes be scary, like at that moment.

"She needs the cool air," Bernadette said.

Unlike her situ, Bernadette and her grandfather weren't close.

"You don't pay the bill for electricity," he snapped and, despite that flicker of fear, he reminded her of a yipping dog, one of those little ones that acted all ferocious until you roared louder and it raced away with its tail between its legs, pissing itself in the process.

She choked down the urge to laugh. Hearing the refrigerator open and seeing who was with Jiddo smothered any temptation for that. It was the Nose.

"Eliosh, please don't be mad," Situ pleaded.

Her grandfather moved to Situ's chair and muscled her up. "You will lie down to stay cool," he said before turning to Bernadette. "And you will go back to your home."

"But—" Bernadette started to protest, the sentence unfinished. What about the game? They weren't done. He couldn't just order her around—that was *her* grandmother. And if he really cared, screw the power bill! Turn on the damned fans and make the woman comfortable! Hadn't Situ already suffered more than enough, considering the biggest of the family's wounds in the tragic legend of Mary?

Her grandparents moved into the front bedroom, then her grandfather closed the door. Bernadette suffered a rush of heat in sympathy—how could he expect Situ to cool off in the airlessness of that room behind a sealed door? But the inferno engulfing her soon evaporated, and only ice remained, for she realized the Nose was staring at her, one of Jiddo's precious cold beers in his mean right hand.

"You have a mouth on you," he said, his voice like venom that was spoken instead of injected.

Bernadette didn't want to but forced her eyes up to record, yet again, the details of the snake who'd sprayed those toxic words. The heat had added a new layer of ugliness to him in the form of sweat and peeling skin on the top of his overly reddened forehead. Not for the first time, she thought of his dark eyes as black. Given what she knew and also suspected, it was easy to imagine those eyes as being fashioned in Hell. Unlike Jiddo, the Nose was tall, hunched. *A refugee from a crypt,* she mused. Clad in work dickies even though he never worked, a dirty undershirt over a flabby paunch, and shoes that looked too new and expensive for such a rancid old demon, the most prominent feature was his big, hooked nose.

Like a bird's beak, Bernadette thought.

"A big, filthy mouth," the Nose grumbled before taking another swig of beer.

Bernadette cast a glance at the closed bedroom door. Whatever help or mercy she might have expected from her true family against this distant devil-relative was gone.

She sucked inward on her lips, making a comeback impossible, and cut across the kitchen, knowing how dangerous the Nose could be. At the door, she let down her guard and huffed, "*Alanif!*" under her breath just loud enough to be heard.

The Nose—it even sounded like an insult in the language of their native land, a world of distant wonders and dangers. And poetic, too, as it rolled off her tongue and ended in a puff of breath.

But the satisfaction proved fleeting.

"What did you say, you little bitch?" the Nose barked at her back.

She heard the muffled thunderclap when he slammed the beer bottle onto the clean counter and the mad scuffle of those shiny new shoes behind her. Bernadette charged through the heat, taking the stairs in a blur. She reached the landing but didn't chance a turn to gauge her progress.

"You mouthy little bitch!" the Nose bellowed.

The couple on the first floor answered in counterpoint, admonishing yet one more upstairs visitor. Bernadette pushed open the front door and fled onto the stoop. The late afternoon heat was double its earlier brutality, and the odor of the Spigot River hung over the neighborhood, smelling like the damp underside of a log.

"I get my hands on you, and I'll kill you," the Nose shouted. "You'll never be anything more than a stupid, worthless girl!"

Tears stung at Bernadette's eyes. She flung open the gate and was back on the sidewalk just as he rounded the triple-decker in his shiny shoes bought with blood money.

Tears for her grandmother, for Mary. And more because of what the Nose said. He was wrong about her, about her potential, and that of young women overall. As she ran along the same sidewalk she'd skipped earlier that day, she vowed to prove it.

Chapter Four

The unmistakable sound of the undertakers reached through our walls. The shuffle of their boots, the murmur of voices, even their occasional laughter as they attended to their work was easy to hear. As they removed the bodies—two from the apartment across the hall—they talked about casual subjects like the weather, the new apartment opening up closer to the start of the Alphabet Complex, and how light the woman's body was.

"Like nothing's there," one undertaker remarked.

I made my father a breakfast of the remaining berries. The chill of the refrigerator had dulled the fruit's warmth, but I could still taste the sun.

"Are you leaving me alone today?" my father asked.

"No," I said.

Every part of me ached. I'd planned to spend the day regrouping, mapping out my next course of action. If the fallen city had been deforested, surely there were other places where edible green things could be found and harvested. The Earth was resilient. It didn't matter that the P.F.R. had relegated all food production to the M.e.A.L. factories elsewhere in the Inner Rings; places that likely stunk of rot. Nature was stronger than those who'd anointed themselves as gods and She would outlast even the Redactors.

I fed my father and cleaned up. Briefly, I thought about washing floors and wiping down surfaces. But then I heard the sanitation crew working in the dead couple's apartment, readying it for new tenants, and my exhaustion doubled, helped along by a dark emotion. I walked my father to the bathroom and back to his sofa, then the twenty or so steps to my own bed dragged out like a distance of kilometers. Or light years.

I imagined them working over there, doing the usual bare minimum: sweeping and disinfecting the floors, kitchen, and bathroom. Nothing too remarkable—they could clean for a week and still the place would be no more welcoming than the two hours spent on preparing it for its next occupants. They only ever repainted if blood was spilled during the previous tenants' demise.

These miserable hovels deserved a match more than any of the valuable things set on fire by the Redactors and P.F.R.

I rolled over. My legs felt calcified.

Lactic acid, the voice in my thoughts shared reminders. *The burn people felt when they used to hike or exercise.* I stretched, my flesh igniting. As painful as it was, my discomfort was proof of life. Proof I hadn't gone grey or foggy like most of the people around me.

I slipped out of bed and checked on my father. He drowsed with the cable plugged into his scalp port, lost in the nothingness broadcast from towers located at the Core of Saturn City.

I checked the cabinets and caught the odor of the open loaf of M.e.A.L. A foul taste bloomed on my tongue. There were a few cans of things, nothing more appetizing than that other putrid concoction. Once a week we received our food delivery for two. It was left at the door and, if you didn't answer the knock, you risked the cardboard carton vanishing into some other neighbor's apartment.

Let them have it, I thought.

Standing at the sink, I wondered what other nutritious treasures had been lost in the green space cropping up over the fallen city. In addition to the berries, I'm sure some of the trees I'd seen were fruit bearing. It's plausible that many of the flowers were edible. If there were bees, that meant somewhere close by there was honey. Birds produced eggs. All those greens, many of them infused with life-giving vitamins and actual *taste*.

I closed the cabinet and stirred the stink of the M.e.A.L. Despair again washed over me, threatening to drag me down into the depths of the hopelessness already absorbed into the filthy floor beneath my soles.

* * *

The usual, single knock pounded the outside of the door, warning that the weekly delivery had arrived. I raised my cowl and opened the door. The cardboard box waited outside, as I knew it would. I bent to retrieve it, only going through the motions. The F.O.G. was killing my father, but the diet they put us on wasn't innocent. I'd decided to attempt to follow the course of the Spigot River away from the neighborhood of old houses; see if that direction led toward an oasis where I could gather greens and other edibles capable of negating my father's condition and to help his body heal from the toxins it absorbed each time I opened a can of processed swill or he plugged into the F.O.G.

The door across the way was already opened, the delivery box left to one side. I considered the likelihood that neighbors would grab up the spoils left behind for occupants no longer there when the scuffle of steps sounded from the direction of the front entrance.

At first, I assumed the two figures dressed in drab olive and old boots were part of the cleaning crew or undertakers there to remove additional corpses from the building. They carried a table—oblong and covered in scratches. The two young men entered the empty apartment.

I picked up our delivery box slowly. One of the newcomers reappeared to do the same. He noticed me and shot me a threatening look, one that warned me to not even think about stealing their food delivery without the need for a single word.

He was the younger of the two youths—brothers, I assumed. In the few seconds in which we exchanged glances, his a scowl, mine one of bewilderment, I recorded his rough handsomeness. My age, I assumed—eighteen, not much older. His hair was dark and one length longer than what would be considered military-short. Still neat, which led me to assume that he and his older brother saw to that facet of grooming in the hope of jumping rings through enlistment. Blue eyes, far from foggy. They were heavy with dark emotion—hurt and what was likely a solid dose of anger.

I noted his long, athletic body, big feet in those old military boots, and undeniable handsomeness. At that moment, I experienced a rush of attraction unlike anything I'd ever felt before and nearly tripped over my own feet getting back behind the door to our apartment.

* * *

I opened the box, knowing the garbage it contained. But while my body went through the motions of putting things away, my mind traveled across the hall. If not exactly eidetic, my memory was near perfect, and I studied the picture my eyes took of his face. I chanced a smile. For all of the pain I saw in his expression, the young man was, well, *magnificent.*

But if he was here, like I, he'd stepped into limbo. I struggled to keep my father alive for the sake and love of a parent, true. Still, there was a selfish component. If Lawrence Bistany died, I'd be evicted from the Alphabet Complex and turned over to the P.F.R. for status review. I was too old for the orphanage, a way station from which all manner of horror stories filtered down from A to choose-your-ending-letter. There, the young were herded, the prettiest selected by Inner Ring P.F.R. families as adopted children, servants, or, according to the worst of rumors, flesh. Regardless of the truth of this or not, if my father succumbed to the F.O.G., I would be unmasked and punished.

I reached a shaking hand to the side of my head where the port implant should have been but wasn't.

"*Situ*," I whispered.

* * *

My thoughts returned to the young man's lips, the lower slightly plumper than its twin on top. In my imagination, they tasted like sunshine when we kissed, mine as sweet as the blackberries that used to flourish near the outskirts of the fallen city. We kissed, and he was masterful not awkward. Shivers tickled my insides. I'd fantasized about other young men before this one, who I'd only seen for all of fifteen seconds, but something about him was different. Foolishly, I wanted to see more of him. Not only unwise, such desires were also dangerous. We didn't know our neighbors. Best that they didn't learn about us.

About me.

I stripped out of my robe and turned on the water. It never got more than lukewarm and it was rationed, so I stepped in without delay and washed. I ran a bar of rough soap over my skin. Little lather appeared. Even so, thoughts of kissing that young man left me aroused. I pleasured myself beneath the tepid spray and bit back my howls as a smaller but no less powerful version of the Big Bang that first gave life to the universe was recreated within my soul.

* * *

I attempted to distract myself as I often did by invoking names and authors of the past, all gone from the world except within the matter of my brain. Then I focused on lost wonders of the ancient world—the Parthenon, the Pyramids of Egypt and the giant stone cat statue of the Sphinx, the Coliseum, Stonehenge, the enormous stone busts of Easter Island, the Colossus at Rhodes who was reported to have stood with legs spread over the entrance to the harbor, and the Great Library at Alexandria.

The Library.

As soon as that thought crossed my consciousness, I forgot all about the handsome, angry young man recently moved into Building R and what I imagined to be the heavenly taste of his lips.

I sat up and faced the mirror, also forgetting how to blink. Movement stirred in the glass. I narrowed my eyes and peered deeper.

"The Great Library was part of a bigger intellectual complex called the *Muselon*—a center of learning dedicated to the Nine Muses," my grandmother said. "At the height of its prosperity, it contained hundreds of thousands of papyrus scrolls, including the works of Hipparchus, the Father of Astronomy. All that he knew was contained within the Library. And all of it was lost when, in 48 B.C., Julius Caesar and his soldiers set fire to boats in the harbor and the conflagration spread, consuming the Library at Alexandria."

She walked out of the mirror and sat on the bed. I listened, as I always did, and rested my head on her lap. As with other visitations, she wore her exuberant dress and a cameo pin. She smelled of flowers from the green spaces in the fallen city and stroked my long hair as she imparted knowledge.

"Of course, they've been burning libraries and attempting to destroy what we've learned from the start—which is why we are here, condemned to this new Dark Age. If you don't learn from history, you're doomed to repeat past mistakes. The Library at Alexandria millennia ago, others containing rare books in Moscow and Buenos Aires only a century in our past. And then the Redactions. Attempting to obliterate truths, sentences, words… burn history and anything *other* that doesn't subscribe to a particular religious or political belief."

Anger boiled in my belly. "We're so small. Up there, there must be a million other planets with a billion stories, all archived and shared from one generation to the next among enlightened races."

"Perhaps." She held a gentle, thoughtful look for a while.

"The universe continues regardless of the P.F.R. and their Redactor puppet masters. Comets leave and return. Stars burn down and go nova."

Her slender but powerful fingers stalled atop my scalp. "I saw the most famous comet that pivotal year. Haley's Comet, which returned from the wastelands of deep space to fill the night sky. And I recall thinking—how many others throughout history looked up and were inspired to do more, *be more*, by an event that only happens once every seventy-five years?"

I turned my face up and studied her beautiful though sad expression. "Will we learn differently by the time it returns?"

The sorrow in the lines around her eyes and mouth deepened. "Who's to say there'll be anyone left when it does?"

We faced one another, and more of that deep understanding passed between us in silence.

"They're looking for the Library," she whispered.

"At Alexandria?"

"No, *Bibliopolis*, the lost city of books. They've been trying to hunt it down and finish what they started for thirty years."

I nodded. "I went to that old house, the triple-decker," I said and sat up.

"My situ's house?"

"Yes. Near the river. The river's mostly gone, but the riverbed's still there."

"That's where it all began," she said. "Because of what he said, what he did to me."

"*Alanij*?" I asked.

Her expression darkened over a barely perceptible nod. "The Nose."

We remained in silence for a spell after that. I resisted the urge to glance at the broken mirror. To do so would reveal that I was seated alone on my bed, speaking to an imaginary friend. Worse, that I was talking to myself, which would prove I was alone in the world, my father a living ghost, even the new young man who'd woken something in me probably just a kind of illusion born of loneliness and want.

My grandmother's hand on my cheek drew me back from fully waking.

"My situ was treated poorly and ignored. I did all that I could for her, but who was I? One little girl with a head full of dreams and stars."

"You're the most powerful woman in the world," I said. "Strong because of your wisdom. And your heart."

She turned my face directly at her. "Palermo, do you remember what I told you?"

I answered first with a puff of laughter. "I remember *all* that you've shared with me, Situ."

She nodded. With her image shifting half in and half out of focus, it was difficult to read her expression. But my little answer seemed to make her proud. "Not about comets or quests—not even about the food growing in the wild that you can harvest to help reclaim your father."

A distant whine sounded. I tracked it to the corner of the room and the grey F.O.G. cable barricaded behind a piece of scrap lumber we'd found in the apartment, more detritus from the previous tenants.

"There is one part of the story I haven't told you, Palermo."

"About Bibliopolis?"

The whine doubled, becoming worse than the buzz of some bloodsucking insect that had latched onto tender skin and more like a teakettle whistle. It wasn't the F.O.G., wasn't in the corner any more. It was inside me.

"*There*, Palermo."

I blinked. The whine shorted out, and I found myself standing in a different room. This one was cool, cavernous, and dark. A strange, sweet smell filled my next desperate sip of air. My imagination translated it into vanilla, though I'd never experienced the real thing. It was also that of museums. I'd never set foot in a museum because such places of learning no longer existed.

"Where—?" I stared to ask, only to catch myself, the lone word in my voice carrying around me with a haunting echo across great distances.

I knew this place. I'd been here before in the most secret of all my grandmother's visitations and stories.

An oculus far over our heads lit the center of the chamber. My vision adjusted and I saw that we stood at the heart of a vast room lined with shelves, and, upon those shelves, were what had to be a million books.

It wasn't the smell of museums, exactly, but of libraries. We had traveled to the largest ever created.

"You know where you are," my grandmother said. "You understand where I have taken you, Palermo?"

"Yes," I gasped. "Bibliopolis—the lost city of books!"

My situ exhaled. That proud smile showed even clearer now, despite the cool shadows that surrounded us.

"Well done, my wonderful grandson," she said.

The whine returned. The vision blurred even as the temptation to reach out and touch the nearest books filled me—oh, my desire to read all I could about great love and the Old West and the stuff of dreams as they once were! But the glimpse into that mysterious realm evaporated, and I found myself back in my room at the Alphabet Complex, alone once more, my flesh electrified with pins and needles.

Fourth Interlude

"Please come with me," Bernadette said. "It's a beautiful day. You need to see the world."

The irony—Situ had seen much of the planet from the Mediterranean Sea to the east coast of America. But the girl was correct in how she sold the day. The heat and humidity had broken and a pleasant taste of New England autumn kissed the city.

"After, we can pick grape leaves—and dandelion greens, too!" Bernadette said.

Her grandmother roused somewhat from her disinterest. "And before?"

"A glorious adventure perfect for two bright, beautiful women."

"*Women?*" her grandmother laughed, though not in dismissal. "Last I knew, you were all of twelve, Bernadette."

Bernadette folded her arms. "You can either trust me and have an outstanding day or miss out on this adventure. I'd say the choice is yours—but it's not, so let's move before the sun sets, Situ!"

Her grandmother grumbled something unintelligible in Arabic beneath her breath and stood. Bernadette caught the sparest smile on Situ's face, a small victory she would build upon.

Situ vanished behind the bedroom door to change out of her housecoat.

"Wear comfortable shoes," Bernadette called. "Part of the fun is that we're walking. Maybe skipping."

Her grandmother emerged ten minutes later in a day dress and flats. Pinned to the dress was the antique cameo Bernadette's father, Situ's eldest son, had bought her for Christmas. Her grandmother looked younger, more alive, than she had all summer.

"Only for the grape leaves," Situ said and winked.

* * *

There were vacant lots and green spaces along the Spigot River where wild grapevines grew. Those leaves that weren't too woody and toothsome could be stuffed and baked, becoming one of Bernadette's favorite Lebanese dishes. She liked stuffed grape leaves, even stuffed cabbage, but her favorite was the stuffed squash that Situ cooked. As for the dandelion greens, one of her fondest memories was of plucking the saw-tooth leaves of the hated weed with her grandmother when Bernadette was only five. Situ had chopped the greens fine, sautéed them in a cast iron skillet, and scrambled eggs and cheese to create an omelet whose memory made the girl's mouth water.

Of course, grape leaves and dandelion greens had been the lure to coax her grandmother off the chair in the living room and out of her sedentary existence.

"Where are we going?" Situ asked on their slow amble down the sidewalk.

"To the castles of Scotland. To the Great Wall of China. To the moon, if you want, my dear," Bernadette answered.

They crossed from Daisy Street to Myrtle and from there to East Broadway, which led past the high school and courthouse to their first destination—the way station and launching pad from which those many other exciting locales could be accessed. The city library was housed in a concrete and glass box that was, to Bernadette, the most beautiful of sights.

"Here?" Situ groused.

"Oh yes, *here*."

They wandered up the cement walkway, passing a water fountain, and entered the vestibule. Beyond the next set of double doors, the air was cool and sweet with the vanilla smell of books—thousands of books. As Bernadette drank in that first breath of the library, she imagined absorbing every word from every book into her cells. The same thought unleashed a chill within her chest. *I want to read every book, every story that's ever been written!* She came out of the trance enough to take her grandmother's hand and lead her into the stacks.

"What do we do?" Situ asked, her voice broadcasting through the solemn silence.

A man seated at a library table reading an open newspaper shushed her.

Bernadette whirled on him. "Don't you ever tell my grandmother to be quiet!"

The man's eyes shot open. Bernadette noticed his throat knot under the influence of a heavy swallow, proof that no further protests would be made.

"What we do," Bernadette said in a softer voice, "is read. Explore. Learn. Evolve."

She sat her grandmother in one of the big, comfortable chairs and returned with a selection of books. One was *Dogs of the World*, a big hardcover volume with illustrations. Her grandmother loved dogs and had had several in Lebanon—though her grandfather refused to let her have one in America. Another of the books was a collection of Aesop's fables. The third was *The Prophet* by Lebanese-American writer

Kahlil Gibran. The fourth was called *Portraits of Lebanon* and contained mostly stunning photographs of the land of their origin.

Situ's eyes widened at the last of Bernadette's recommendations, and the girl regretted the choice. She attempted to draw the book off her grandmother's lap, but Situ held onto it.

"No," she said.

Bernadette nodded. "I'll be right back." She left to give her grandmother time to compose herself, maybe sneak a private look at the book and sink into good or sad memories.

Bernadette made the usual rounds through the children's room, taking some books that should have been behind her but weren't because she loved their whimsy, their stories. Along with Dr. Seuss and the animal tales of Beatrix Potter and Rachel Runge, she grabbed other books that should have been beyond her reading level but weren't. One was a dog-eared paperback copy of Mary Wollstonecraft Shelley's *Frankenstein.* Another was an ancient hardcover with black and white photos from distant lands. *The Moon: Our Nearest Neighbor* completed the stack filling her arms. Feeling both excited by and proud of her selections, Bernadette marched over to the vacant chair beside her grandmother. The book about Lebanon sat unopened on Situ's lap.

"You don't have to read that one," Bernadette whispered. "I just thought… but the beauty of it is, you can read as many other books as you want."

Situ's scowl deepened. "No, I want this one." She gripped the book, drew in a cleansing breath, and opened the cover.

Bernadette sucked down her own deep breath, then flipped through the hardcover to page 474, to a picture she knew and loved. It was the Marmite in Southern France, a gargantuan rock balanced between mountain peaks left behind by receding glaciers during the last Ice Age. As the planet had warmed, the glaciers deposited this massive stone on its lofty perch. The black and white photograph showed the Marmite rising above those peaks, its top covered in tall pine trees, the entire presentation resembling that of an ancient, fallen city.

How could you be a person of this world and not be amazed by its wonders?

Almost as humbling, Bernadette glanced over and saw Situ lost in a similar daze as she eyed the cedars of Lebanon and other visions from that lost life. The spare smile was back on her grandmother's face. Most telling was the happiness in Situ's normally sad brown gaze. Bernadette had promised an adventure to transcend time and space, and she had delivered.

* * *

She checked out the maximum number of books permitted on her library card and stowed them in her backpack, which also contained plastic bags for the second part of their day's adventure. After a light lunch at a sandwich shop on the corner of East Broadway and Canal Street, they wandered back in the direction of Daisy.

"Try it, Situ," Bernadette urged.

Situ made a face, but her smile betrayed her willingness. "No, I can't."

"Sure you can."

"I'm too old."

"You are a beautiful and strong woman. You can do *anything*—certainly skip!"

Just when it appeared the argument would end in defeat, Situ skipped. The movement was awkward and inelegant but also wonderful to behold.

"That's right, Situ," Bernadette sang.

She skipped beside her grandmother, and, together, they continued toward the green places along the banks of the Spigot River.

CHAPTER

FIVE

Dandelions. Mushrooms. Grape leaves—if I found the leaves, chances were also good I'd locate fruit. The wild grapes would be sour, but I could temper them by boiling them down with a small amount of sweetener. The mushrooms would substitute nicely for the putrid meat scraps in the M.e.A.L.—I just needed to be sure I harvested the edible varieties. Dandelion greens were bitter but loaded in nutrients. I gathered up bags and tucked them into the inner pocket of my cloak.

I checked on my father, who sat up and brooded on the sofa.

"I don't want you to go, Pal," he grumbled.

"I know, but it's the only way I can get the things you need."

"I don't want them," he spat.

Had he the energy, I imagined my father stomping his feet and tossing a tantrum. I recalled my grandmother's words about him being the child now, me the parent, and suffered more of the melancholy that I was always trying to stay ahead of.

I cupped my father's cheek. Scowling, he turned away. There were days I had no patience, when I wanted to stomp my feet, too. Worse, to rage against him and shriek into his face, calling him out for his childish behavior. I never did, because on most days, I understood his anger toward me was a gift—proof that he hadn't given up.

"Wait for me," I didn't ask but demanded.

He grunted a response.

"Do you need to go to the bathroom?"

Avoiding my gaze, he was beyond adult conversation. I was the baba now, he the child. I leaned forward and kissed his sweaty forehead.

"I will be back as soon as I can. Remember—do not get up on your own. You can be as mad at me as you want when I return, but don't hurt yourself, please."

Turning, I left the apartment.

I walked into the dark hallway and navigated it as I always did, assuming the identity of a daughter, not a son, to the eyes of the outside world. None of the residents here cared much for their own lives, let alone the stories of others. I'd worn this disguise for my entire life except in my father's company. It was a comfortable second skin, as involuntary as blinking or breathing.

I moved past the door to the new neighbors' place, and my thoughts returned to the handsome youth. As I continued, I imagined him in there, caring for a single parent or two who'd grown foggy enough to be sentenced to the Letter R. A strange emotion blossomed in my stomach. Only after I was out in the greyness of that early morning was I able to identify it as a kind of common ground with another human being. Kinship with a stranger who didn't know me.

* * *

Traces of the aches from the long hike stung at my leg muscles. There would be fresh reminders by the time I returned, I guessed.

I walked in the direction of the access road running behind the Alphabet Complex but didn't get far before the sound of voices alerted me to the fact I'd been noticed. At the rear of the building where the makeshift basketball court and sad remains of picnic tables were located, a small gathering of young men in this land of the old and dying was engaged in a game of two-on-two. I ordered my gaze to remain low on the ground, but my eyes betrayed me.

I knew all about the old sports—baseball, ice hockey, football, and this game, also known as hoops in the lost vernacular. What was taking place was a classic game of shirts versus skins. The two young men on one team wore shirts to identify their partnership, while their opponents had stripped down to bare torsos. I didn't recognize the two shirts—as stated, we didn't know our neighbors. They were older than my age if I had to guess, dirty, their hair long, their shirts wet with sweat. The other two, the skins, were the pair of brothers I'd seen moving into the apartment across the hall from us.

They were sweaty, too, but different in appearance because all that fresh perspiration added to their attractiveness. Especially the younger man I'd seen during our brief encounter on delivery day. I risked a direct look and drank in the image of his handsome face, his neck and upper chest red from exertion, the thin line of hair dissecting him down the middle of his abdomen, his fur-ringed navel, and the way his drab olive cargo pants and old boots fit him in a way that still looked fresh and alive, as though his clothes loved him.

But in breaking that law, I incited *his* notice.

"*You*," he barked, his voice deep—it would have struck my ear like music if not for the threat it contained. "You, *girl!*"

I lowered my head and continued forward, my heart in a gallop for different reasons.

Stupid, stupid, my inner voice chastised.

He grunted something to the others, and I heard the tired basketball bounce off the concrete, imagining it hurled in anger. A scuffle of bootfalls sounded at my back.

"Let it go, Hunter," another male huffed—the older brother, I assumed. "Come on, let's finish the damned game!"

Hunter. That name inspired another emotion, one not so new: fear. I cursed my foolishness, but the footsteps caught up to me. A hand gripped my arm and spun me around. I faced Hunter, now as afraid of him as I was excited by his nearness. I caught his masculine scent on my next desperate gasp for breath—musky and bitter but also arousing. A clean note accompanied it, something that reminded me of the green in the meadows surrounding the fallen city. I imagined it was testosterone, pure and earned, rising up through his skin as a result of the game.

"Were you looking at me?" he demanded.

I shook free. "No!"

"You're lying," Hunter spat. "I saw you!"

Using peripheral vision, I eyed his expression while pretending to be looking at the ground. He was still handsome and smelled intoxicating, but whatever desire I had for him evaporated as he flashed an arrogant look and shook his head.

"You're a whore," he said. "And I bet your mother's a whore, too!"

Rage surged up from my gut. I didn't care that he was a male and I, in my disguise, was expected to be subservient to him. I hated him in that instant. The words raced up my throat, ready to be expelled like vomit. I no longer worried for my safety—let him expose my deception, let it all burn. Everything that mattered already had! The fury I experienced toward this hateful prick could not be contained.

Then, curiously, a chill washed over me. I swallowed down my response and calmly, meekly answered, "My mother, like so many others, was murdered during the Massacre. And your mother, who I'm sure is a lovely woman, would be ashamed of you for saying such disgusting and disrespectful things."

His hauteur flat-lined, too, and a hurt look replaced his arrogance. It was as if I'd struck him hard across his face.

He fixed me with a stare, stunned by my words. Boldly, I met the gaze of his blue eyes. Hunter blinked first and backed a step toward his brother and the shirts.

"We gonna finish this or you planning to swing your dicks around all day?" one of the shirts called.

I resumed my march down the road, just an inferior female headed toward cinders and death.

* * *

The putrid odor of the fire pits assaulted my nostrils then burned inside my lungs. Something worse filled my gut. I don't know why I expected a son of the Alphabet Complex to be any different from the rest of the world. Hunter's name suited him. He was mean, ruthless, and ugly. My only consolation came from knowing my words had been as precise as the weapons carried by the soldiers of the P.F.R. I'd cut him with my delivery. There was that, I supposed.

The pits.

The dead forest.

All around me was devastation.

By the time I reached what had been the outskirts of the fallen city, my insides ached from a sense of loss. But the image that greeted my eyes threatened to consume me.

The city had attained new wounds. Parts of it that had been standing had collapsed under the bombardment from the troop transports. All of the green was gone, incinerated. I was looking at a modern recreation of battlefields from the past, a kind of new Redaction. Only instead of books and history, the Redactors had torched all of the green life, preventing those condemned to the

Alphabet Complex from growing healthy or escaping the inevitable slow death sentence imposed upon all in the Outer Rings.

* * *

I sat on the dry bank of the Spigot River. Something buzzed near my ear. My instinct was to swat at it, kill the offender, but I couldn't bring myself to steal even an insect's blood as my tears spilled, at first unable to be stemmed.

Composing myself, I stood and faced the old triple-decker. The sad house brooded beneath massing storm clouds. I wandered away from the dry riverbed to the shattered pane of the main door set beneath the portico. My focus settled on the glass. Between the fractures, a shape took form.

"Situ," I said.

"I know you feel lost. Hold on, Palermo."

The tears resumed. I stopped fighting them. Finally they waned on their own. When I blinked and could see again, I found myself back inside the shadowy stacks staring at a million books all neatly lined upon shelves.

"The Library," I gasped. "*Bibliopolis!*"

"Take my hand," my grandmother said.

I did, knowing the strength contained in those deceptively frail fingers.

She led me through the stacks. I drank in the titles—encyclopedias, dictionaries, and books on learning foreign languages. Farther along were volumes devoted to the natural world, astronomy, and geology. I spied a special title—*Dogs of the World* among them. Memoirs. Novels. Short story anthologies. An untold number of truths and fictions, stretching in every direction.

"Is this real?" I asked.

"Yes, Bibliopolis is real," she said.

We passed a window. I released her hand, backtracked, and stole a long look out at a courtyard framed by a mix of Doric, Ionic, and Corinthian columns. A water fountain geysered at the center. Other buildings of elegant stonework and glass loomed beyond. On one structure, the gentle smile of a gigantic sundial face stared back, no bursts of light or shadows telling the hour.

"*The Lost City of Books*," I gasped.

My grandmother nodded. She took my hand again in hers and we resumed walking, passing many rooms, some vaster than the one already crossed. We entered a space filled with glass-front cases, rolling metal ladders that ascended to shelves located far over our heads, and wooden columns capped by exquisite carvings of acanthus leaves. Carrels lined the heart of the room along with comfortable-looking chairs upholstered in merlot velvet.

My grandmother led me to the chairs. We sat.

"If it's real, let me return with my baba, Situ—we'd have a safe haven to live free from the P.F.R. and their Redactor masters!" I implored.

My grandmother's expression saddened. "Do you know where we are, this particular collection?"

I looked around. Titles were impossible to read, the volumes ancient, elegant. I shrugged.

"This is the Rare Book Collection, the oldest and most valuable of all the billions of texts stored within Bibliopolis. It could be argued that every book here is rare. Yet here, we sit surrounded by the history of the ages—all that has ever been learned and dreamed and written down by the human race."

A chill teased the fine hairs at the nape of my neck. Unable to halt it from tumbling, I gave in. The shiver fell down my backbone. A tingle possessed my whole body. "So all was not lost in the Redactions? Bibliopolis prevailed!"

"Access your memory, Palermo. Recall what you know about heritage seed repositories."

I did. My mind traveled to frozen wastelands at the top of the world, to vaults constructed deep underground beneath the surface. "Seed banks—collected and stored should there be any global threat to the environment like a nuclear winter or impact from an object in near-Earth proximity like a comet or asteroid."

"What you see around you is a version of that principle applied on an extensive scale to books. This lost city is all that remains of the efforts of those of us who saw what the Redactors planned and prepared for a future when they would die out along with their ideologies, hatreds, and influence."

The library surrounded us, silent apart from our voices. In the absence of other sounds, my thoughts came clearly—so clearly that I wondered if I was even speaking or projecting words through telepathy.

"That hasn't happened," I said or thought. "The Redactors haven't gone away, nor have their puppets in the P.F.R."

Situ leaned back in her chair and fixed me with a look through narrowed eyes. "Why do you think that is, Palermo?"

I understood that she was again challenging me. The unknown number of stories she'd shared with me dating back to my earliest memories came with follow-up questions meant for me to exercise my brain.

"Including the words, destroying and absorbing the knowledge changed them. They ingested the ashes of history after burning the entire world."

"Yes, that's true," she said. "But wouldn't absorbing any number of religious texts or the words of Pearl S. Buck or the Beat Generation poets enlighten even the deadest of hearts? The belief that the Redactors are still walking around in a naturally sustained form, still capable of inflicting so much cruelty on this world they obliterated, is a common falsehood, like believing the world is flat."

I choked down a dry swallow and wondered if the sweet vanilla smell of the books was hypnotizing me. "You believe there is a another explanation?"

"I know there is. The Redactors are no longer human as we know the meaning," she said. "They should be dead by now, lost to their graves. And yet they continue to prowl the Earth and unleash fire. Why is that?"

"Something concocted in the P.F.R. laboratories in the Inner Rings or the Core? Better nutrition or medicine?"

"Those are solid explanations, though none of them exactly works. Try not to over-think the obvious. A select group of former humans kept alive decades after death should have claimed the last of their miserable carcasses. Where would they get that kind of energy?"

Frustration gripped me. She knew the answer but expected me to voice it. I normally loved these tests, because I knew they expanded my consciousness. I readied to fire off a comeback full of quick speculations but froze.

"If the Redactors are cheating death, living beyond their time," I whispered, the words sour on my tongue, "they must be stealing that life and lying about it. That's what Redactors do. They lie and they steal."

My grandmother's sad smile returned. "Now, you're beginning to truly understand."

My next breath hitched in my throat. "The grey F.O.G. All those people connecting into it... *dying*. They don't know that at the other end, the Redactors are plugged in and stealing their lives!"

Fifth
Interlude

They rinsed the greens then Situ chopped them, showing grace and finesse with the knife despite arthritic hands. Then they worked on the grape leaves, carefully patting them dry on paper towels before Situ used the knife to remove wooden stems and veins. She blanched the leaves, filled them with the mixture of ground beef, rice, crushed tomatoes, pine nuts, and spices, rolled them into little pillows, and lined them in a covered baking dish.

The dandelion greens with eggs and cheese were exquisite, made even better because they ate them with what Bernadette called Situ bread—fresh pita buttered and toasted atop the open flames of the gas stove's burner. They savored the stuffed grape leaves wrapped in the same bread, un-toasted, and washed the divine meal down with lemonade.

"You are a good girl," Situ said, smiling from the other side of the table.

"And you are a great woman, Situ," Bernadette said. "The strongest one I know. You're my role model. I want to be just like you when I'm older."

Situ's smile sagged, and the sorrow returned to her gaze. "It's getting late. But this was a fine day."

Bernadette wanted to say more, to invoke the name of the young woman mentioned in whispers in her grandparents' home, the daughter who never arrived from Lebanon, the one they'd trusted the Nose to shepherd. "Let me do the dishes," she instead said.

"No," Situ protested.

"Then we can see the comet—the sky tonight will be perfect for viewing!"

"Comet? I'm tired, granddaughter."

Bernadette rounded the table and kissed her grandmother's forehead. "Then you get comfortable while I clean up. You rest and nap. Promise me you'll get up to view the comet knowing I will be watching it at the same time in front of my house. No arguments."

Situ flashed a tired smile. Bernadette cleared plates and cleaned the kitchen. After checking on her grandmother, who had nestled beneath the covers in her bedroom, Bernadette picked up her backpack and headed down the stairs.

The door to the apartment on the ground floor was closed—one unwanted encounter avoided. She resisted the urge to backtrack up the stairs and descend a second time like a horse or to slam the front door. After all, it had been a wonderful day.

She exited into the late afternoon's golden light. The city's air smelled sweet, the weight of the books hanging off her shoulders barely there. If she could, Bernadette would have filled the bag twice as full. Ten times. She imagined herself checking out every book in the library, lugging them back to her room, and being surrounded by piles of adventures and millions of stories. On the sidewalk, she resumed skipping.

Bernadette was so lost in the joy of the moment that she failed to notice the man hastening up from behind until his shadow fell over her. He reached down and seized hold of her backpack's shoulder strap and whipped the girl around. Gasping, Bernadette looked up and into the hated face of the Nose.

Rage filled Bernadette, but the emotion quickly shifted to terror after he grabbed at her collar and dragged her off the street and through a vacant lot running close to the bank of the Spigot River.

Chapter Six

The terrible truth left me paralyzed. The F.O.G.—often, I'd wondered why maintain the Outer Rings at all? The P.F.R. had culled down the population to numbers that could be controlled, but I'd always questioned why they'd stopped with mothers and grandmothers at the Massacre on that day of bloodshed and sorrow. Now I understood the answer. They needed the castoffs, the cattle, to support the Redactors, who fed off the life energy drained by the insidious device. They needed a recurring supply of mindless slaves for sustenance. My stomach lurched.

I returned from the visitation to discover I was standing on the front stoop of the old triple-decker, staring into the fractured windowpane.

"No," I said, my voice sounding alien in the wasteland of devastation that ran as far as the oceans and beyond—to Lebanon, to the moon, and to the ends of the solar system.

I wanted to go back to Bibliopolis, to the books, the knowledge, and the safe, sturdy walls. But I was once more in the ugly world made by the Redactors.

* * *

In an overgrown area not far from the remains of the river, I found wild morel mushrooms and gathered them into a bag. The air smelled dank and green but with a note of deceptive sweetness. I discovered grapes growing across the remains of a fence. The fruit was as sour as I expected, though ripe, so I added handfuls into my growing list of spoils. Dandelions sprouted, most of the flowers already turned to seed. I plucked leaves and gathered them in bunches. While following the old course of the river, I came across a tree that had dropped large shells. Cracking one open on a rock revealed the meat of a walnut. I gathered up as many as I could.

My bags bulging with the healthy produce, I turned back in the direction of the Alphabet Complex.

My mind wandered to forced marches and desert journeys of the distant past. I recalled that some of our ancestors had crossed land bridges and the ice from eastern Asia to the Americas, tracking big game while trying to beat out the advance of the glaciers. Surely, I'd walked a thousand miles—or so the ache in my legs claimed. But what about my visit to the lost city of books? That journey must have been even longer, one thousand light years and through folds in time.

Thoughts of the grey F.O.G. sickened and infuriated me. So, too, did the image of the Alphabet Complex, the uppermost floors of two of the buildings close to the end of the line rising to view in the last of the daylight. The rancid stench of smoke from the fire pits stung at my nostrils. Ignoring the pain, I walked on, a familiar worry filling me over not knowing what I would find upon opening the door to our apartment.

* * *

My father was curled on the sofa and plugged into the F.O.G.

My anger surged again along with the temptation to rip the cable from his head. I grabbed hold of the connection. The grey F.O.G. pulsed in my hand. I imagined that it was an asp filled with venom and readying to strike. But the serpent was far deadlier than a real cobra. Willing my fingers to relax, I released it and shook my father awake.

"Dad, I'm here," I said.

He came back from the emptiness preying upon him and sucking away his life, his eyes unfocused at first before seeing me. "It's about time."

"I know."

"You've been gone too long. And all this time, I've been here suffering," he chastised.

I helped him to stand. En route to the bathroom, he added to his list of complaints. "Where's my dinner?"

"It's on its way, I promise."

After the bathroom, I opened bags and examined the bounty brought back with me from the ends of the Earth. I sautéed the mushrooms and walnuts, blanched the grape leaves, and did a poor man's modern interpretation of the Lebanese dish. I cooked the greens and added the sour grapes, blistering them in the pan. I presented the meal to my father.

"What's this?" he demanded.

"A taste from the past. It's *life*—now eat up," I said.

He did, cleaning his plate.

"Is there more?"

I nodded and served him seconds. That question sparked some hope; I just might be able to save him. While he ate and I cleaned up, a knock sounded at the door. The lightness I felt from seeing my father eat healthy fare died, smothered by panic. No one ever knocked except for the weekly food delivery, and those that visited apartments in this

Alphabet usually did so by kicking in doors like they had with the medicine woman.

Holding my breath, I waited for a second knock. When one didn't sound, I forced my legs into moving and opened the door. No one stood outside. The air was pungent with the foul mix of cooking odors and an indelible residue of sweat. I wondered if neighbors might detect the proof of my illegal food preparation through that noxious haze and decided no—*nothing dreamed up in our apartment can overpower that stew.*

As I was about to close the door, I noticed the object left outside—a single can on the floor, just beyond the threshold. From the cut of my eye, I saw the movement of the door to Hunter's apartment close.

A peace offering? I picked up the can—beans in brown gravy. It wasn't much of a gift, and yet it felt like the best ever given throughout all of human history.

I placed the can on the dresser beneath the mirror's lightning bolt scar and studied it from my bed, aware of my smile. Maybe Hunter wasn't the utter jerk I'd labeled him earlier in the day. If my words had affected him, that meant there was a soul beneath his magnificent but brusque exterior. And a heart. I rolled onto my back and lost my gaze in the dirty ceiling and its gridwork pattern of acoustic tiles.

"*Hunter,*" I whispered, loving the feel of his name on my tongue.

Numerous scenarios played out, my thoughts projected onto the ceiling along with a thousand words. In the first, Hunter, dripping with sweat from his game of hoops, apologized for his disgusting insults by taking my hand and kissing its palm. His next kiss blessed my lips—gently to start but firmer, more intense as our connection deepened. In the next, we sat together at the picnic tables, the game of basketball over, only the two of us there. His shirt was still off, his sweat dried. Hunter nudged one of his big, booted feet toward mine, an action as playful as it was thrilling. "I'm sorry, Palermo," he said.

I allowed myself to indulge in the fantasy and really relax for the first time in years. Only after I imagined the two of us walking the empty, elegant streets of Bibliopolis did I surrender to the truth. Hunter didn't know I was Palermo. To the world, I was *Palerma*, a girl. So even if he had any attraction toward me, it was misplaced and doomed. We all were here.

Sitting up, I eyed my reflection past Hunter's peace offering and watched a scowl replace my smile. He couldn't know—either about my true gender and identity or about the big secret I harbored within me.

I picked up the can and entombed it in the kitchen cabinet with the others.

* * *

Still, the dreams…

I saw Hunter and I in the rare book room reading copies of first editions and journals written by hand in actual ink. Of course, this came after I taught Hunter to read. P.F.R. signs contained visuals, not words. English had become mostly a spoken language—and the only legal tongue, even if parlayed badly. When the last of my father's generation was gone, so, too, would be the written component.

We read there to each other, the only living souls in Bibliopolis. Our days were filled with intrigue, mystery, and love. Surrounded by the millions and millions of books, and through their authors, we filled our minds with all there was to know, our souls with knowledge, and our hearts with celebration. We made love in every room in the city, and we were happy.

I woke in the gloom just after dawn. As the drab and familiar borders of the room surfaced from the night, it struck me that it was reasonably possible that Hunter hadn't left the peace offering after all. It could have been his brother's doing over embarrassment. Few things were certain in the Alphabet except for F.O.G. and death. The time for foolish dreams was over. It was another morning in the Outer Rings.

* * *

I was the baba again.

"I want you to stay away from that thing," I said, tipping my chin at the wall cable.

My father finished his meal. "Why?"

"Because it's evil. It is killing you. Every time you plug your mind into it, the evil drinks your blood, feasts on your flesh, and devours your soul."

"And what am I supposed to do instead?"

"Be with me. Talk. Tell me things I don't already know about the great Lawrence Bistany."

At first, my words amused him. Not long after his little smirk blossomed, my father's expression tightened. "You'll go away again and leave me alone."

I shifted on my knees at the side of the old sofa, believing my muscles would pop and my bones crack from the misery of the long miles they'd endured. "I am all yours today, Dad. I'm not leaving you."

After two healthy meals of clean, natural food, he was more present than he'd been in months. His face relaxed. "What do you want to know?"

"Tell me a story about when you were my age," I invited.

My father's unshaved throat knotted under the influence of a heavy swallow. "The summer I worked at the restaurant. The war had only just started—"

My thoughts circled back to the conflict that had broken out to then burn across other parts of the globe before engulfing our backyards. *War*—there'd been so many, the reasons all so stupid when you factored losses measured in blood.

"—and I didn't know if we were going to be drafted into service," he continued. "It was a little place, not one of those big neon franchises. I started by bussing tables. Then they let me work in the kitchen washing dishes. After that…"

"You learned how to cook," I said.

"Yes. Have I told you that you do a very good job?"

I laughed. "I could never be as good a cook as you, Dad."

"You didn't taste my food at the start of that summer. I'm lucky they didn't fire me."

It was a familiar story, maybe the only one my father remembered anymore.

"One night, I got an order—for a *croque monsieur*. Fancy ham and cheese sandwich that's fried golden brown with an egg on top. You eat it with a knife and fork. The trick is for the egg to be over easy, so that when you cut into it, it covers the sandwich like a luxurious sauce. Only the customer complained to the waiter that her egg was too medium. That—"

"It didn't run," I whispered.

"So I remade the order and carried it out myself, and when I got to the little table for two near the window, sitting there was—"

"The most beautiful young woman in the world."

Tears stung at the corner of my eye. Worse was the sadness that broke in my father's expression, his misery unable to be released because he'd already shed all the tears inside him.

"Your mother, Diane," he said.

A terrible silence fell between us, the story's recital over.

"I'm tired," he sighed.

My father reached for the F.O.G. cable. I intercepted his hand.

"No," I said.

"I can't sleep without it."

"Try."

I helped him to stretch out and kissed his head. The bitter smell of his hair again sent my tears falling.

* * *

I knew the story of how they met in the restaurant, how he messed up her order, fixed it, and the spark that resulted. How they dated and married even as the books burned, eventually taking the world with them. How I was born closer to the start of the Alphabet. The Massacre on Mother's Day, when I was hidden in the woods as those woods died, too. How they lied and acted to keep me a secret, disguising me like a girl so that no one would see I hadn't been scarred with the F.O.G. implant like everyone else; easier to do under the hood and capes the women had to wear.

"Because you are special, Palermo," my grandmother said in my thoughts. "You needed to be protected."

I caressed my father's cheek. The flesh around his scalp where the implant dug into his skull showed the usual irritation, a mild case of F.O.G. fungus in the form of a few crusty, raised scabs. My father pulled away and turned over.

"I can't sleep without it," he tsked.

"No," I didn't urge so much as order.

He huffed out a breath. I stood, made it over to the kitchen sink, and splashed water on my face. *Special?* I supposed so. I could read. I knew scientific and mathematical facts none of my fellow hard timers did. A million-million stories were archived in the matter of my brain—the ancient mythologies of the Greeks, Romans, and Norse alongside the legendry tomes of William Shakespeare, Lord Byron, and O. Henry. I could recite the stories of Mark Twain, the poems of Gerard Manley Hopkins, and the adventurous mysteries of Sir Arthur Conan Doyle. But at that moment, I didn't feel particularly special.

A footstep sounded outside in the hallway. I didn't think much more of it than proof of some neighbor coming or going. But then knuckles wrapped lightly on the door, our unknown caller sounding less sure of his reasons than I felt special. My mind returned to the can of food left the night before.

My heart galloped.

I approached the door, cracking it open a few inches.

Hunter stood beyond the gap. I drank in his magnificence—his face so handsome in the poor light and sour atmosphere of the no-man's land of the hallway, the way his olive button-down shirt, drab cargo pants, and old boots fit his body in a way that should have been criminal. Unable to stop myself from so brazen an act, I faced him through the cover of my cloak, loving the blue of his eyes. More so, his nervous grin, made all the more attractive by the scruff of five o'clock shadow showing on his chin, cheeks, and throat at this late morning hour.

"Hi," he said.

I nodded and attempted to hide my own joy from his blue gaze.

"You got what I left? I'm sorry. It was a real dink thing, what I said to you. I'm not a dink. I hope you know how sorry I am."

"Your apology is accepted," I said.

So he *had* left the food to atone for his disgusting behavior and words. That answered the biggest of my questions and eased most of my doubts. However, he was still a stranger, still dangerous. The conversation with my father about my late mother, only minutes over, was the perfect reminder to keep doors closed and my guard up no matter how heartfully sorry the handsome young man appeared.

Bowing, as was expected, I closed the door. Once it was shut, I braced the door with my spine, aware of the speed of my pulse and the tingle inside my belly. The gentle knock sounded again. I hesitated. No footsteps testified that my handsome visitor had left. I waited. Long seconds later, I cracked the door open.

Hunter hovered out there looking even more nervous.

"I wish you'd give me a chance to prove it. That I'm really a nice guy," he said.

Oh, how those tickles grew even more mischievous, rippling outward in concentric circles like the surface of a pond in the rain. The shivers consumed my entire body.

"I have to care for my father," I said in a meek voice.

Hunter shrugged. "My brother Rex and I take care of our dad. Maybe I can help you with yours."

"No, we're fine. Thank you."

"Okay. But if you ever want to talk…"

"Talk?"

He shifted his weight from one big foot to the other and flashed a spare but stunning smile. "Sure, I'd like that. There isn't a lot to do around here. Gets lonely just staring at the walls."

He laughed, but the sound was laced with madness. At that moment, I saw he was as lost as I was, as lost as the rest of the world.

"Where would we talk?" I asked.

Hunter's eyes widened with hope. "We could sit outside in the back, you know, on those old tables."

I nodded. I glanced at my father, who remained restless but was losing the fight against sleep.

Five minutes later, as promised, I joined Hunter at the line of broken picnic tables, and we talked.

Sixth
Interlude

The afternoon went dark, the eclipse helped along by the false dusk of the surrounding green space. Bernadette screamed. Pain exploded across her cheek. The bastard's smack knocked her to the ground. She tasted dirt.

"You miserable little *aikalba*," the Nose spat, using an insult from their native tongue. "You think you can talk to me with such disrespect that I won't punish you? *You*, a worthless girl?"

Along with the dirt, Bernadette tasted the metallic tang of blood, an indication of just how hard he'd struck her. Tears welled in her eyes, but she ordered them to stop and mostly succeeded.

"*You're* the little bitch!" she fired back.

He lunged at her, and this time she was ready. Bernadette pitched a handful of dirt at the monster's face as he dragged her up from the ground by the strap of her backpack. The Nose stumbled several steps in retreat after releasing her and covered his eyes. He howled like an injured animal. Bernadette dropped her shoulders and the weight of the books inside eased the backpack down. She swung the makeshift weapon, nailing him in the meat of his paunch. The Nose doubled over clutching at her backpack, his eyes wide and wild.

"I'll kill you!" he shrieked.

"Like you did Mary?"

That truth, hurled for the first time directly at the criminal, struck the Nose with the same efficiency as her attack to his gut. The monster looked away.

"I didn't kill Mary!" he said in a voice that had fractured.

"She never arrived! You were supposed to protect her. My situ trusted you! Instead, you broke her heart, you ugly, rotten excuse for a man!"

She tried to retrieve her backpack. The Nose recovered enough from his shock to be able to hold onto it and the library books it contained. Then the Nose made another grab at her. Bernadette avoided his fingers with their long, dirty nails.

As he scrambled back to his feet, his shoes no longer so shiny or new looking, it struck Bernadette how much danger she faced. The Nose had dragged her to the river's edge for a reason. A chill cut through the heat of her anger and satisfaction at having inflicted wounds as part of an overdue defense.

"You are a hateful, evil man," she lobbed at her attacker. "I'll tell on you, and you'll pay for what you did to me—and when you die, you'll burn in Hell for what you did to Mary!"

The Nose seemed to remember the backpack still in his clutches and tossed it toward the Spigot. Her backpack and the precious library books struck the water. The Nose stepped toward Bernadette.

Bernadette ran.

And ran.

* * *

With her lungs on fire and the twilight a blur through watery eyes, she listened for the scuffle of those shoes now covered in river dirt, but they never came.

Bernadette's heart seemed determined to jump out of her chest and onto her tongue. She slowed, and it continued to pound around the inside of her ribcage like a nervous, trapped animal. Never before had she been so terrified, so certain that her life was in jeopardy. He planned to kill her—Bernadette was sure of it!

Nothing looked familiar. She had run so fast, so far, that Bernadette had arrived at a different city, one far from home. Somewhere in Lebanon, perhaps.

The terror kept under control spilled out and poured down her cheeks as tears. Already struggling for breath, her next hitched in her throat. The wonderful day with her grandmother was part of a different life, one now ended. Going forward, she sensed the world had changed and that the story of Bernadette would now be defined by Before and After Attempted Murder at the hands of that vile man.

She'd called him out on his evils for what he did to her and especially Mary. But the victory was bittersweet, because Mary was still gone while the Nose walked and drew air and continued to commit his atrocities. Bernadette wiped her eyes on the back of her now-dirty sleeve. A street sign materialized on a telephone pole. Park Street. A recognizable landmark! She could follow Park down to the common, get onto Hampshire and through the vacant lot where the giant red hollyhocks grew, and, from there, turn onto Exchange Street. Their ground-floor apartment wasn't as distant as she'd feared.

Another small victory, this one, too, was doomed to be brief.

The two-story, beige box appeared, visible in the glow of the streetlamps. Bernadette hastened down the sidewalk, fearing that she'd forgotten how to skip—worse, that she might never again considering the weight life had dropped onto her back since the last time she'd danced along the pavement. Home—her mom would be there, likely worried over her lateness. Her father, too. Good, because she'd tell them all that had happened, all that the monster with the hooked nose had done to her.

She approached the house, put on a burst of speed, and charged up the driveway only to dig in her soles and stop.

A second car was parked beside her father's, a long black sedan she'd always found ugly.

It was the Nose's car.

Chapter
Seven

Long ago, in a little corner restaurant that no longer existed, my father met my mother. Their connection was instant and endured until the madness of the world intervened. A handsome young man had invited me to share his company, and I wondered if, like my parents, he and I would share a similar connection. A few steps shy of the dilapidated picnic table, I realized we couldn't.

Because I was a lie.

By then, Hunter's magnificence possessed me. I mentally resigned myself for a lifetime of unrequited love. I knew I would never be able to forget him.

He sat in a jaunty pose atop the table, his big feet on the bench. Not lost on me was the observation that he'd undone the top two buttons of his fatigue shirt, the skin of his upper chest hairless beneath the prickle of scruff on his throat. I smelled his scent of clean, male sweat and loved it.

Following rules both spoken and unspoken, I sat on the bench, my eyes aimed at the ground.

"Come up here," he said. "I don't really believe in that bullshit about how girls should act."

I shook my head. "Thank you, but it's better that I don't in case someone sees us. I don't want trouble."

Hunter laughed, though not in a dismissive way. "You already proved that you've got more balls than most of the men from H to Z by giving it right back to me."

More balls. I chuckled, too, at the irony. His nearest foot shifted. Hunter climbed down, making us even on the bench.

"Again, I'm really sorry for what I said."

"You've already apologized. I believe you."

"It's just… I dunno, the game. And I was mad. We were up in Building J before this, and then, with no warning, they told us we were moving to R. Our dad isn't that foggy. We could have stayed where we were."

The frustration was clear in his voice. I sensed the words he spoke were long overdue; that they'd been trapped inside him for days fermenting, souring, threatening to grow cancerous if he didn't expel them.

"That's the People's Free Republic for you," I said, not bothering to disguise my disgust. "They're great at destroying the world. Not so good at anything else."

I sensed Hunter's gaze on me. "That's the ballsiest thing you've said yet. The kind of talk that gets people killed."

"Do you plan on reporting me?"

"No. *Hell, no.* I just meant…" He sucked down an audible breath. "You're the only good thing about living here. And I hate the P.F.R."

I tipped a look up from the corner of my cowl. The wounded gaze I'd noticed earlier in his eyes was back and twice as clear. The temptation to embrace him gripped me, and I knew he'd welcome my hug. But I resisted.

"Hunter," I whispered, speaking his name like a magic spell.

"You said you lost your mother—back in the Massacre," he continued, those blues locked with my browns. "I'm so sorry. We did, too. Rex and me. I was too young to remember. But he told me what happened to her. How they walked in and separated all the moms, all the grandmothers. Took them… there…"

He aimed his scruffy chin in the direction of the dead forest.

"You were right—she'd be ashamed of me for saying what I said to you."

I dared not hug him, out here where the danger of being seen was palpable. But I inched my hand closer to his. My left pinkie brushed Hunter's right. He reached over, took my hand out of sight in his beneath the table, and held on with the proper degree of pressure.

The connection had been made, and I'd never been happier.

We remained that way for what could have been seconds, minutes, or hours—time had lost cohesion, and neither of us acted to break the hold.

"Hunter Jones," he said.

I came partway out of my trance. "Nice to meet you, Hunter Jones. Thank you for the proper and official introduction."

"And you?"

"Palerma Bistany," I said—I *lied*.

"That's different," Hunter said.

"I'm different. *Special*, I've been told."

He chuckled again, the sound light and welcome following our shared spell of mourning. "I like it, Palerma. And I already know you're special. You're smarter than most of the dinks I've met, including my brother. You know a lot of words, some of them big. It's kind of intimidating."

Pride briefly gripped me. Hunter was right—I could answer him in numerous languages, quote from any number of classic books of literature, and regale him with stories of wonder, adventure, and mystery. But that was hubris, foolish and dangerous, so I gulped it down.

"Your brother," I said, changing the subject. "That's Rex? Rex Jones?"

"Yeah. He's got some stupid plan to enter the P.F.R. recruitment pool. Says that if he gets selected, he'll have us back at the start of the Alphabet, as high as B or maybe even A Building. Or that if he does really good, he'll make it to the Inner Rings. Won't listen to me when I tell him they don't recruit Outer Ring dinks into the city's Core. He thinks he's doing it for our dad, but he only cares about himself."

I could gauge by the anger in Hunter's voice that he truly hated the P.F.R. My grip on his hand tightened. This brought us back eye-to-eye.

"There was a world before them, before the Redactors and the fire they unleashed," I said in a voice barely above the whisper mark. "There will be a world after their time. Empires rise and fall, and tyrants turn to dust."

"But how much blood has to be spilled until then?" he asked.

I couldn't answer as my mind attempted to add up all the blood—and ink—already paid in sacrament to the rulers of Saturn City.

Hunter's fingers tightened around mine. He shifted closer, stirring his magnificent scent. I breathed in his smell, loving it. But an instant later, I detected the charred fetor from the burial pits, and I knew it was time to go.

I rose from the seat. Hunter held on.

"Meet me again," he said. "Please."

I nodded. He released me. I returned to the apartment, elated at the thought of us as a couple and torn by the terrible truth that one of us was a lie.

* * *

I imagined Hunter, stretched out on his back in a jaunty pose, arms behind his head, a blade of Timothy grass clutched between his teeth. He smiled. He was happy.

In my mind, we had traveled to the green shelter of the fallen city before the P.F.R. enacted their scorched earth solution. He'd removed his shirt. The flesh of his torso shined in the sunlight. A drop of sweat glistened in the trail of dark fur cutting him down the middle.

Lowering, I kissed him fully on those incredible lips. He cupped my chin and nestled against me after our mouths parted.

"I love you, *Palermo*," he growled.

I was naked in the sunlight, honest. He knew.

He accepted.

I eased into the protection of his hug and curled up against him to rest my head on the furry nest under his arm. Above us, Earth's moon was visible in the blue noon sky, its face full, close, and stunning.

"That biggest impact crater, it's called the Mare Imbrium," I said, pointing up. "That other one is the Mare Serenitatis and, there, the Mare Tranquillitatis."

More hubris, I know. But this was my fantasy.

"What happens now?" Dream-Hunter asked.

I pondered his question. "Somewhere out there, hidden from the Redactors, is a lost city. A city filled with books."

"Books?"

"Everything that's ever been written down, ever known, ever imagined as possible. A city filled with knowledge."

"Where is it?"

"I'm not sure. I've been there a few times in what I think is an astral sense. Through telepathy. In visions."

Dream-Hunter fixed me with a look. "Why does this city exist?"

"To protect everything we know, all we've ever dreamed, from being obliterated."

He sat up, leaned over me, and set his other hand on my cheek, caressing my lips with his thumb.

"But Palermo, *why* was Bibliopolis built?"

The moon towered over Hunter's head like a halo against the bright blue sky. I pondered the question. Was the lost city of books only designed as a repository, a museum? Or was it meant to function as a true library where books could be read, checked out, and the knowledge contained within distributed?

"Palermo?" Dream-Hunter prodded, his voice no longer so attractive but dusty, like the puff of something flammable that had just been set on fire.

I glanced from the moon to my handsome new friend. Hunter's sapphire blues were gone, replaced by sockets stained with cinders. A Redactor held me in its embrace.

I trapped the scream behind my teeth and bolted upright in my bed. Hunter... what I felt for him was so wondrous and exciting. But the situation was too dangerous, and I decided that my father's safety and my own were more important than any chance at happiness with the attractive young man from across the hall.

* * *

I fixed my father his morning meal and set it in front of him. While he ate, a knock sounded on the door. I knew the identity of our caller.

My heart galloped. I faced the door but didn't answer. The knock repeated.

My father looked up. I held a finger to my lips, urging silence. I was the baba now, it was established, so he listened. A footstep creaked on the hallway floor. Our caller departed.

"Why didn't you answer the door?" my father asked.

"It isn't wise, isn't safe."

"You don't know who it was."

"But I do. Now eat, Dad. You need your strength."

I cleaned up the plates. My father reached for the grey F.O.G. cable.

"No," I snapped. "I told you, no more!"

"What am I supposed to do?" he fired back.

"How about we go for a walk?"

* * *

We had lived in Building R for three years. The move was the last time I saw my father walk anywhere other than within the confines of that foul apartment, a distance that stretched from the sofa to the bathroom. I wasn't sure he could make it down the hallway to the front door now, but even the effort would benefit his health.

"Come on—the air isn't exactly fresh, but it's better than sitting here in the same spot," I said.

I dressed my father and helped him on with his old shoes, which had sat discarded in a corner long enough to accumulate dust. Holding onto his arm, I walked him into the long, dark hallway. We passed the door to the Jones apartment, and I worried—and hoped—it would open. It didn't.

At first, my father's steps were shaky, so I almost turned us around. But nearing the exit, he walked with just a little more confidence. We passed outside and into the somber morning, our amble fated to be short because of the threat of rain.

"You should have answered the door," he said as we plodded down the fractured sidewalk, the impediment of apartment buildings stretching ahead of us to the horizon. "It might have been important."

"It wasn't. How do you feel?"

My father held up his chin. A trace of the regal man he'd once been before plugging into the F.O.G. surfaced. I saw the person he'd been in that other life before the full horror of the People's Free Republic stripped away most of what mattered. He answered me with a curt nod.

"When we return, do you want to shave?" I asked.

He considered my question. "Maybe. We'll see."

It was a small show of defiance, his telling me he was still the baba, I the child. I laughed. So did he.

"I think this is far enough. Let's turn around," I said.

"No, a little longer, please."

"All right."

I indulged him. We continued forward under the shadow of Building P. The first drop of rain struck my hand. The storm had arrived.

"That's it for today. We can do this again," I said in my most diplomatic voice.

My father hesitated. The rain fell. I turned him around, and we faced the misery of our only shelter. Walking faster, I looked up. Building R seemed to recede farther away, taunting us with a lure of false protection.

Halfway across the distance, he fell, taking me down with him to the wet ground.

I recovered and attempted to help him up, which I'd done numerous times when he slipped in the apartment. My father howled—from pain or rage, I couldn't tell which.

"Dad," I said. "Can you stand?"

Before he answered, I caught a flash of movement from our periphery.

"Here, let me help you," Hunter said.

He pounded over to us, his boots splashing in the new puddles. I looked at him, admiring his athleticism, his grace. With Hunter's help, we lifted my father back to his feet.

"Mister Bistany?" Hunter asked.

My father nodded. "And who are you?"

"A neighbor," Hunter said. Then he shot a glance my way. "A friend."

I wanted to believe it, and I certainly could have, given the care in which he assisted us back to the front entrance.

The rain spilled in a deluge. I caught Hunter's scent, his sweat and skin mixing with the downpour to become something even more magical. Not lost on me even in that moment was how gently he handled my father.

We returned to the building. Its dank smell killed the scent of Hunter. All three of us bedraggled, we entered the hopeless ground-floor apartment.

Hunter slipped off his boots inside the door and stood in a pair of drab socks, his big right toe poking through a hole in the threadbare fabric. We shepherded my father over to the sofa. He sat and flashed a mischievous grin.

"What, Dad?" I asked.

"That was fun. We will do it again."

Hunter laughed. I wanted to laugh, too, but my insides had tightened into knots. More, I longed to trust Hunter. I desired him. But I couldn't allow myself to be vulnerable to him. To anyone.

"I'll get you a towel, Dad," I said and retrieved one from the bathroom.

I dried my father's face, finished, and turned to Hunter.

"Thank you, Hunter."

"No problem." Then, in a lower voice, he added, "I wanted to see you."

I spun away from him. "Maybe another time."

He set a hand on my shoulder. "You're wet, too. You should change. After, can we talk?"

"No," I said. "Goodbye, Hunter."

I walked off before he could press me, waiting for the sound of his boots—again on his feet—walking out of our living space. Instead, the floor creaked behind me.

"Palerma," he said at my back.

Hunter stepped closer, right against me. I gazed down to see his big feet in their old socks on either side of mine.

"You're drenched," he said, his voice warm against my cheek. "If you don't get out of these clothes…"

He took hold of my cloak and lifted my disguise.

Seventh Interlude

The last of the day's warmth evaporated. A chill stuck to Bernadette's sweaty skin. *His* car—the ugly land boat that reminded her of a hearse. The Nose was in there spreading more lies, these about *her*.

She retreated away from the driveway and back onto the sidewalk. Turning, she continued with her eyes aimed ahead, the world at the periphery dark and blurry. There was nowhere safe to go. Then, shivering, she caught sight of a glow in the sky.

Haley's Comet, she thought and thawed.

Up there, at perihelion, traveling between the planets Venus and Mercury. It was a once-in-a-lifetime event. More than that, *a sign*.

Bernadette resumed walking and followed the comet's lead.

She pressed forward, aware of the distance traveled in her bones but not stopping until she caught the white glare of the building's lights and heard the tumble of water. The latter seduced her ear like a child's laughter. She marched past the fountain and through the vestibule doors. Beyond, into the cool, vanilla-scented calmness and, from there to the front desk.

"We're just about closed," the librarian said over her shoulder, not facing the late arrival.

Bernadette cleared her throat. "I have something to report, ma'am."

The librarian remained with her back to the girl. She wore a salmon pink skirt and matching blazer that lent the woman a boxy shape. Staring at a computer screen, she answered. "Please make it brief."

"A man took my books," Bernadette explained in a monotone voice. "They were in my backpack. He pulled me down to the Spigot River. I fought him off, but he threw my backpack with my library books into the water. I think he planned to murder me."

In a disconnected way, Bernadette impressed herself given the precise delivery of that report. The woman turned. She wore her hair short, and the librarian's head looked square, adding to her boxy appearance. Her eyes widened behind her glasses.

"What did you say?" the librarian asked.

"I'm so sorry about the library books. I'll do whatever I can to replace them. I have a birthday coming up, and I always get money from my situ—that's 'grandmother' in Lebanese-Arabic."

The librarian raised the drop-down counter shelf and moved beside her. "Are you all right?"

Bernadette nodded. "Yes, I saw the comet. I..."After that, her memory of events jumbled. She had a vague understanding of the librarian guiding her to a chair in a room that smelled like buttered toast and microwaved dinners. Then of a policeman dressed in his dark uniform with the long-sleeved shirt.

"What's your name?" he asked.

"Bernadette—though I always wanted to be Lemise after my grandmother. That's her name in Lebanese-Arabic. It means, 'God touched her.' I just think that Lemise sounds beautiful. Though she doesn't like it because it sounds like, lemons—'three for a dollar,' she often jokes."

"This man who attacked you," he asked. "Do you know who he is?"

"The one who killed Mary—she was my father's big sister. I call him 'the Nose' because he's got a beak for one. He doesn't like that. It's why he tried to murder me down near the river."

There came a break in her memory after that, a void in which time and space got tangled and everything went dark. When she woke, she was in an emergency room bed, both parents and the policeman surrounding her.

"Yes, I want to press charges," she heard her mother say, her voice rising to a shriek.

"If you don't, I'll kill that son of a bitch myself," her father said.

Bernadette never saw the Nose again after that night except in her nightmares.

* * *

She skipped into the kitchen and picked an apple out of the fruit bowl. The first bite exploded across her taste buds crisply, the flesh firm, the perfect balance struck between tart and sweet. Bernadette swore she could taste the sunlight and the autumn on her second.

"I'm gonna bring one of these over to Situ," she said and picked up another of the apples.

Her mother, nursing a tall mug of coffee at the table, spoke her first words of the morning. "No, not today, Bernadette."

"Why not?"

"Your grandmother isn't feeling up to company."

"She never does. That'll change once I get her out for some fresh air."

"I said no," her mother snapped.

After it happened a second time, Bernadette suspected it wasn't Situ who didn't want company but her grandfather, who'd forbidden her from visiting as punishment for sending the Nose away.

* * *

The square woman was Mrs. Finley, and she welcomed Bernadette for two afternoons following school and every other Saturday to help out in the library to cover the cost of replacing the books. Not that the fault was Bernadette's—Mrs. Finley made it clear that Bernadette bore no responsibility. Their time, however, was mutually agreed upon and offered Bernadette a chance to overlook being denied the hours she would normally spend at the triple-decker with her grandmother.

At the library, she shelved books, learned the Dewey Decimal System, and, above all, read.

Though thinking herself aged past such childish things, she entered the children's room and approached the shelf with the special books. She selected three. Such wonders, she decided, weren't only designed for kids but could also be appreciated at any age, even that of grandmothers. Seated on the big blue sofa with its pattern of little pumpkin orange, sunny gold, and cherry red squares, she opened the first book. A T-rex unfolded from between the covers in 3-D, terrifying detail. She imagined a child half her age squealing in surprise and smiled. Another flip, and the thick pages exhumed a pop-up Ankylosaurus with its armored bowling ball tail. The next, and a Diplodocus attempted to unfurl, only some nitwit kid hadn't closed the book properly and its tail had gotten snagged. Bernadette corrected the injustice, and the docile giant rose from between the covers once more.

A soaring Pterodactyl. An Allosaurus. Every flip of the page was an adventure, every popup a surprise. After that book, she moved on to the planets. Opening the second book sent Earth's moon out of the creases, full and close enough to touch. Mars and Saturn, Jupiter with its red storm eye, and the Earth, most beautiful of all in the solar system, followed. Finally visiting cold, tiny Pluto she closed the book and reached for the last precious hardcover sitting on her lap.

Energy sparkled through Bernadette's insides as she worked open the cover. From the flat, dimensional curves, a 3-D version of Paris popped up, one complete with the Arch de Triomphe, the Eiffel Tower, and the Louvre Museum. London was next, easily identified by Big Ben, the infamous Tower, and bridge. Tokyo, Cairo, Sydney, and Mexico City rose from between the covers. Last, she reached New York City. The Empire State Building soared out of confinement, flanked by the Brooklyn Bridge and the Guggenheim Museum.

Bernadette stared at the wonders in front of her. When she came out of the trance, she closed the popup book and made her journey through the cities a second time.

* * *

She studied Library Sciences and graduated to a job waiting for someone of Bernadette's enthusiasm. At twenty-nine, she married Theodore Bistany. Two years later, she took over for Mrs. Finley when the head librarian retired.

Not long after that, the trouble began overseas. Over the next decade, it spread, resulting in the first of the homegrown conflicts soon to be known as the Redactions.

Chapter

Eight

I set my right hand over Hunter's. His nervousness telegraphed up through my palm.

"You're beautiful," he growled into my ear.

I leaned closer. "You don't know that."

Hunter nodded. "I do, Palerma."

The words were past my lips before I could trap them. "I'm not who you think!"

"Then show me. Let me see the real you."

"No, Hunter."

"You're special. I know it, too. I…"

His voice trailed to a sigh, but his praise had already flattened my defenses. Special? For my entire life an apparition from a broken mirror had told me I was different, *special*. I knew some of that claim was true. I was a keeper of secrets, of stories, of knowledge and lost history. It was more than just a very good memory. Even as words wrote themselves across that blank section of bedroom wall in passionate red strokes, I acknowledged that I was also fragile and horribly lonely and, at that moment, my judgment lapsed. I removed my hand from Hunter's and leaned back against the side of his face. He removed my cloak. Undressed of my disguise, I turned to face him, feeling naked both physically and in matters of the soul.

My cloak dropped from his hands. The silence in the room pulsed, the air almost too heavy to breathe.

"What—?" he asked as his eyes traveled over my body, seeing a flat chest and a cock where none was expected.

"My real name's Palermo," I confessed. "*Hunter…*"

He broke focus and moved past me, all of the youthful excitement gone from his face. I spoke his name again. As the red words bled and vanished, he continued his retreat. I imagined him stopping long enough to retrieve his boots, and then he was gone.

I stood frozen to the spot. The secret I'd harbored from everyone save my father and a ghost was out. At any second, the P.F.R. and their Redactor puppet masters would descend. I'd jeopardized our lives for no reason other than the desire for a handsome young man's affection. Was it any wonder we'd come to this dark time in human history?

Were all people as weak as me?

Dressing, I returned to my father. I wiped his hair again and helped him out of his damp shirt.

"Where's your friend?" he asked.

"Gone."

* * *

"You need to remember this, Palermo—they've been searching for the lost city of books for a very long time," my grandmother said.

We slowed our pace and found ourselves standing beneath the giant sundial whose face smiled despite all of the dangers that surrounded it and Bibliopolis.

"The Redactors and their People's Free Republican puppets— they'll go to any length to locate and destroy this place."

No sunlight or shadows tolled the hour. The sundial appeared to be frozen in time. I inhaled. The still air lacked the freshness I expected from so vast and magical a place.

"Why?" I asked. "Where does their hatred for books originate?"

"In one lie that fractures into others. There's a core group that perpetrates the lie for reasons of personal gain—wealth, power, or satisfaction of ego. Others who are rudderless... *rootless*... listen and believe, finally thinking they've found a purpose. Desperation becomes zealotry. Suddenly, there's only one acceptable belief system, one truth. Everything else is a reason to go to war, to cancel out, to set aflame. No difference can be tolerated. If a truth doesn't solidify their position of power, then it is destroyed; be that truth a government, a person, an idea or a book. And they are all found here. In this city of books," she sighed.

We turned away from the sundial to face all the buildings and collections housed among a fantastic architecture of carved friezes, obelisks, and arches over walking paths.

"Preserved here are over 132 million books, all that were known to exist in the world before it was ignited during the Redactions. All that we knew, everything that we were, captured in words. Those words have strength, Palermo. They could change the course of the future. This city must be protected!"

I shook my head. "What's the use? Why bother?"

I realized I had, for a second, become my father, grey and foggy.

"The use?" my grandmother repeated.

"If everyone's dying, feeding life into the Redactors, if nobody cares anymore..."

"Do you care?" she challenged.

"Of course, but..."

She folded her arms. My situ was a diminutive woman in stature, but her size was deceptive in terms of her power. She was formidable and had endured even the dark events of the Mother's Day Massacre. Our gazes locked. She softened from her defensive posture.

"You mean the boy?"

"I risked everything, Situ. I'm not special—I'm stupid. I willingly removed my disguise for someone who doesn't care about me. The *real* me."

My grandmother took both of my hands in hers. "Do you think yourself unworthy of being loved?"

I looked away. Her grip tightened, hard, which brought us back eye-to-eye.

"You are, Palermo. Love is a big part of what makes you special. You deserve love and to be loved. And love is a very necessary key in protecting this place from those who would destroy it."

She took me in her arms. I gazed up at the sundial's face, so happy despite the unhappiness that had led to its creation. Bibliopolis sat in silence around us. I thought of the millions of voices contained within the city's walls—Victor Hugo and his hunchbacked hero, Melville and his white whale, R.E. Dent and her Janus demon—and wondered why ours were the only ones speaking. As soon as that thought crossed my mind, the contours and boundaries of The Lost City of Books blurred, and I found myself once more alone in my room.

* * *

"Eat, Dad," I said.

My father grumbled, now on his second day of being denied access to the F.O.G. "I need—"

"You need to eat and not create more worry for me," I said.

I kissed his forehead. A knock sounded at the door. I whirled. In my mind, P.F.R. soldiers were massed in the hallway having received a lead that could help them locate the lost city of books. Then I remembered knocking wasn't their style. I choked down a dry swallow and opened it slowly.

Hunter stood outside, his eyes heavy, his appearance that of the guilty.

"Hi," he said.

"Hello," I answered.

"Can we talk?"

* * *

We sat on the end of my bed.

"I'm sorry," he said.

I didn't respond. For the second time, I found myself forgiving him for his behavior.

"It's just that…"

"No, you didn't know. If anyone should apologize, it's me to you," I said.

He reached for my hand. "Don't. Let me finish. I liked you, Palerma… *Palermo*," he stressed. "That hasn't changed. In fact—"

Hunter reached over, lowered my cowl, and studied my face. A wide smile broke on his lips. He leaned closer and pressed his mouth against mine. I thawed and kissed him in return. Not long after the connection, his tongue tested my willingness. I opened my mouth and accepted his gift. The joy was back, my worries mostly gone. The kiss continued, sweet and hungry in equal measure.

When we parted, Hunter took my face in both of his big hands and rested his forehead against mine. "I was attracted to you. I'm even more into you now; you're so brave."

I listened, inhaling his scent, loving his touch. Boldly, I eased my hand between Hunter's legs and found him hard. Hunter moaned his approval. We kissed again.

"You can't tell anyone," I said. "Promise me, Hunter. You can't tell anyone what you know!"

He nodded. "I won't. But why? Why walk around living like a female?"

I resisted the urge to remind him that I was special. He'd already come to that conclusion on his own. Instead, I reached up and swept aside my locks, showing the unmarked patch of scalp beneath where every other person under P.F.R. rule bore the receptor port from which the Redactors secretly sipped the force of life. Hunter uttered something not quite a word. He set two fingers on the side of my head and gently felt along my skull.

"Where is it?"

"It isn't."

"How—?"

"Does it matter?"

Hunter lowered his hand. I fell into the hypnotic pull of his blue gaze and surrendered more of my heart to him. I could have stayed in that moment, a tiny slice of time, forever.

"During the Massacre on Mother's Day, they hid me in the dead forest. With all of the blood being spilled, the Redactors and the P.F.R. overlooked one tiny, screaming baby. After that, I'm told, my father continued to dress me as a girl so no one would notice me. So I'd be invisible."

Hunter blinked and came back from whatever thoughts had transported him far beyond my small bedroom in the Alphabet Complex.

"I noticed you," he said. "And you're *beautiful*."

He crushed his mouth over mine. I indulged in the taste of his kiss and the scent of his nearness. Saying nothing, Hunter toed off his boots and unbuttoned his shirt. My excitement built, fueled by the clean, masculine smell of his skin and fresh sweat. For a confusing second, I wondered if I was still fantasizing, creating yet one more story to record within the protective walls of Bibliopolis. Shakespeare had penned his famous romantic tragedy, *Romeo and Juliet*. Mine would be *Hunter and Palermo*... I liked the way it sounded in my racing thoughts as he removed my cloak, leaving me naked and vulnerable once more before him. Only I couldn't envision how this story would progress—we were presently in the opening pages of the first act.

"*Beautiful*," he repeated while kissing his way down my neck to the hard point of my right nipple.

There, he gently suckled, the teasing pressure from his teeth driving my buttocks up from the bed and blankets. I imagined myself levitating off the Earth, floating like a nimbus cloud, my body transforming from flesh to light. Only his mouth kept me grounded.

So often, I'd asked why—why had I survived past the Mother's Day Massacre when so many hadn't? A level of guilt had followed me around like an unwanted second shadow. Now, with Hunter, that stain was gone. I'd lived to know such human happiness. My flesh tingled with electric pins and needles. I gasped his name.

Hunter released me. A proud grin spread across his mouth, crooked and supremely attractive. I cupped his cheek, loving the scrape of his scruff, before my touch traveled lower, following the contour of his chest and then picking up the trail of dark hair cutting him down the middle. I gripped Hunter's stiffness. Together, we undid his belt and zipper. He stood. His drab camouflage pants came off along with the last of our inhibitions.

I drank in the vision of his legs, athletic and hairy, so masculine, and of his big feet when he peeled off his socks. Even Hunter's feet were attractive in a way that part of the male anatomy wasn't normally considered. He gave me a tip of his chin and flashed his mischievous grin, granting me permission to remove the last stitch of his clothing.

Remaining on my knees, I tugged down his underwear. Hunter stroked my head while I brought him to climax in my mouth. With his nectar painting my lips, we kissed. He guided me onto my spine, feasted on my most sensitive and private flesh, and then entered me, his hardness thick and demanding of more.

My discomfort grew, but Hunter reassured me it would pass. True to his claim, pain transformed into pleasure. I held onto his face as he thrust, and our mouths grew desperate for one another. In my mind, I imagined us as an all-male Yin Yang connected by Hunter's cock. My first orgasm erupted a few seconds shy of his second. In that glorious though paltry sum of seconds when the cosmic effulgence of light and energy consumed me without burning me alive, I thought of Oscar Wilde, Quentin Crisp, D.H. Lawrence, Allen Ginsberg, and so many other male writers who'd loved other men and written about it with such passion.

"I love you, Hunter," I confessed, unable to trap the words behind my teeth.

Our bodies still connected, his face red and soaked in sweat, Hunter collapsed on top of me. "Me, too, Palermo," he growled in my ear.

We remained in that position, his sweat melding with mine on the bunched bedclothes.

He rolled off me, a dreamy look in his eyes. "That was amazing," he sighed. Then Hunter chuckled, the sound joyous, muffled, wonderful.

I placed a hand over his navel and traced the ring of fur until he flinched.

"Stop that."

"No," I said.

"It tickles!"

He squirmed, drew me back into his embrace, and kissed the top of my head en route to claiming my mouth. We made love again. After that, he dressed.

"I have to get home and check on my family," he said and fastened his belt.

In the dim light, the bare flesh of his torso and feet embossed our surroundings with rare hope and happiness. He hadn't yet left, and already I missed him.

As though sensing this, Hunter leaned down and kissed me. "See you soon," he said, and then he left.

* * *

The sun set. While my father drowsed, his belly filled with wholesome food sourced from the Earth, Hunter and I sneaked out to the tables at the back of the building.

"I have trouble sleeping at night," he said, his voice low as dusk deepened.

We held hands under my cloak. I dared to imagine what nights might be like in bed beside Hunter. Would making love still his restlessness, or would I become an insomniac, too?

"I want to go away from here. Far away," he whispered.

I pointed up to the sky. A few stray stars appeared through breaks in the endless clouds. "That's Vega in the constellation of Lyra."

"Huh?" Hunter asked.

"And that one's Sirius in the constellation of Canis Major—also known as the Dog Star."

He laughed, keeping the volume low, almost hidden as we faced the new night.

"And that bright one is Rigil Kentaurus, also known as Alpha Centauri from the constellation Centaur—our nearest neighbor in space. Maybe we could go there."

I sensed him studying me and reveled in the joy of Hunter's fascination.

"How do you know these things?"

I shrugged. "I just do."

"What would we find up there on our nearest neighbor in space?"

"Three stars. A bunch of rocky exo-planets. No Redactors or their puppets."

He nuzzled the side of his face against my cheek. I moaned, loving the scrape of his scruff, the smell of his skin, and, most of all, *him*.

"Sounds perfect," Hunter said.

I had been aching for him from the moment he left my room. Unable to resist though we were in public, I greeted Hunter's lips and held on, not wanting the kiss to end.

"Let's go to Alpha Centauri together," he said.

I loved him. I told him so. The Earth turned in its orbit, and the stars rose as they had for billions of years.

One star considerably newer broke out of the constellations and tore across the horizon. The roar of its engines drove us apart. We turned to see it decelerate and approach from the direction of the fire pits.

"Troop transport," Hunter growled.

We hurried off the table and around the building. The transport touched down between Buildings Q and R. At the front entrance, we stopped and watched a dozen armed soldiers disembark. In the lights of their troop craft, a tall shadow trailed the teal and charcoal uniforms, a wraith that seemed barely there. As it neared, I recognized the Redactor. It wore a monocle.

The walking nightmare from the fallen city turned from the soldiers under its command and looked in our direction. Despite the distance, I sensed its icy version of an eye trained upon me and its false telepathy slithering around just inside my head trying to dig in deeper. The Monocle and I faced one another. Time froze, and seconds transformed into much longer sums. I remembered to breathe and the clock unstuck. Then the Redactor with the monocle signaled to his troops. Two of the soldiers separated from those moving toward the nearest Alphabet building and, together, they and the Monocle marched toward me.

Eighth Interlude

She quietly applied for and won grants. Books arrived in crates or one at a time. Some bore the smell of smoke.

"We're going to run out of room," Bernadette's assistant, Carlos, remarked.

"If we have to, we'll build another library to house them," she said. "An entire city if that's what it takes."

It struck her that her heart was in a constant gallop, a state it hadn't known since the night down near the Spigot River when that hated man had attempted to kill her.

She patted Carlos' shoulder. "Keep an eye on things. I'll be back in five."

Bernadette carried the vintage hardcover, a collection of mystery stories anthologized by Alfred Hitchcock, into the former conference room that had become the library's center of collecting and assigning every book ever published for conservation. Books were stacked dozens deep. It was only the beginning but it was a solid effort.

In the staff lounge, she pulled her tote from its secret hiding place in one of the lower cabinets and checked her phone. Three missed calls from Ted and another from Lawrence waited. Bernadette's next breath came with difficulty. She dialed, aware that her hand shook and of the constant echo of her heartbeat when she put the phone to her ear.

"Bernadette," Ted said, and she instantly sensed his panic.

"What's wrong?"

"We're at the hospital. Diane's—"

"I'm on my way," she said, calmness washing over her in a cold wave that allowed Bernadette to go on automatic.

She returned the phone to her tote, pulled out her car keys, and walked back to the front counter.

"Carlos, there's been an emergency," she said, the volume of her voice set at its usual level of library-low. "I need you to take over and do what's needed."

Carlos nodded. "Of course. Can I do anything more?"

"Keep our library running," she said and, just as calmly, turned and marched out of the quiet oasis and into the city's warmth and loudness.

The hospital. There was something wrong with the baby.

Not again, please, she thought.

Bernadette's next breath hitched with a sob. She choked down her rising worry and continued past the water fountain and to the staff parking lot.

She approached the hybrid and fumbled the key into the lock. As she did, a shadow reflected in the window glass. Bernadette whirled. The man had snuck up on her with the focus and silence of a cat.

"Bernadette Bistany?" he asked.

Bernadette's shock passed enough for her to record the man's features—mostly bald with a few wild grey wisps at the sides of his face, long legs, jeans ripped over one knee. Her first impression was that he must be one of the homeless who sometimes slept on the benches in the library's courtyard or harvested half-smoked cigarette butts out of the sandbox ashtray near the front entrance.

Her surprise passed. She straightened and met the man's pale blue gaze.

"You are the head librarian, correct? The one who's been gathering up copies of every book ever published as the world spirals closer to madness and ashes?"

His line of questioning again shocked her. Homeless, no. He didn't look like the kind of insane follower of the various groups that had pulled together and were calling themselves a litany of different, hateful names; all of them linked by the same insane dogma—the Proud Believers, the Right Militia, and the People's Freedom Caucus, the later responsible for much of the evil being perpetrated here and overseas.

But you couldn't judge by appearances anymore.

"I can't talk to you now. I have a family emergency," she said.

The man exhaled. "This is important. It's about the books. About what you're doing."

A jolt of fear slithered past her exterior defenses. Bernadette pulled the door open and got in. The man leaned closer to the window.

"It's imperative, Bernadette," he barked through the tinted glass. "I'll be waiting for you!"

She thumbed the ignition button on the dashboard. The hybrid's engine purred. Bernadette put the shift into reverse and backed out, not caring if she ran over the man in the process. If he was with People's Freedom Caucus, she could live with the bloodshed. A million times that wouldn't match the crimson deluge they'd already released.

The city passed by with maddening slowness. Traffic lights intentionally turned red between her car and the hospital, adding to the misery in her gut. Bernadette parked in the emergency room lot then rushed through the automatic doors into the reception area. The families of patients beyond the nurse guarding the front desk huddled on blue plastic chairs. A flat-screen television ran on low volume from its perch on a length of beige wall.

She scanned the room. Ted sat alone, his feet in their old shoes flat on the polished linoleum floor, his body sagging in defeat. He looked up, and she saw the terrible truth in his eyes.

"Ted?" she gasped.

Ted stood. For the first time in their many years together, he looked frail, old. She took him into her arms. They didn't speak. Behind them on the television, more images of the fires and devastation, the brutality and genocide, played out. In the white noise ringing in her ears, Bernadette failed to make out which city and country was being ravaged on this day. Not that it mattered—the imagery could have come from anywhere. And everywhere.

* * *

Diane looked small in the hospital bed, and Lawrence had aged almost to his father's years according to the weariness in his expression. Bernadette willed a smile onto her face for their benefit. Mostly, that worked, but the rest of her expression didn't cooperate, which resulted in what she guessed was quite the lunatic's grin.

"Hi," she said, her voice low and solemn.

Lawrence stood from the chair beside Diane's hospital bed and hugged his mother. "Ma," he said.

For the first time in a long while, Bernadette struggled to find the correct words. What was she to say? Everything, especially platitudes invoking anything religious, would sound empty and flat. *You both can try again*—only how much disappointment and pain could Lawrence and Diane endure? What they'd already lived through had broken them.

"I'm sorry," Diane said in the absence of other dialog.

Bernadette came out of her spell of thoughts. "Sorry?"

"I know how much you wanted to be a grandmother. To be called *situ*."

All of the tears she'd kept under control spilled from Bernadette's eyes and down her cheeks. She moved to the side of the bed, leaned down, and kissed Diane's forehead.

* * *

Along with the gallop of her heart was the emptiness inside her that grew, feeding on the misery of the world that surrounded her at close range and the one at large where small fires had started but nobody acted to put them out so that all of the conflagrations were linking together into one global big burn.

She pulled into her parking spot at the library and sat there, staring out through the car's windshield but seeing something other than the patch of empty asphalt beneath the cold white glow of the streetlamp.

The parking lot became a blank page in her imagination. Her mind typed words onto it.

Today, the world ended. A child died, one who might have grown up and shown mercy to his fellow citizens. Instead, the ones with hearts and brains conceded more of their influence, and the ones with no souls and hateful agendas seized greater power. We stand on the edge of a very dark age, and here one insignificant old woman is buying up books and making a stand. I am so very tired.

The words appeared, faded into light greys, then vanished, becoming asphalt once more. Bernadette's tears resumed. She wanted to howl to the limits of her lungs and readied to expel the primal scream, becoming a modern interpretation of Allen Ginsberg's famous epic poem. But beyond the veil of her tears, a single letter reformed.

She wiped her eyes and discovered the letter was a man. A tall, thin man with a mostly bald head dressed in ripped jeans and old shoes.

He crept over to the driver's side window and leaned down.

"Bernadette, I'm so sorry to push the issue, but I really need to speak with you. It's important. A matter of life and death."

Chapter Nine

I saw the Redactor—the same one I'd escaped in the fallen city. Worse, this time it saw me.

Hunter's boots pounded at my side. Most of the building's residents would be plugged into the F.O.G. and oblivious to what was happening. But I'd gotten my father off the habit—was that part of why the P.F.R. and these ghouls were here?

Or was it because of a bigger prize? One as valuable as Bibliopolis?

My fear doubled.

"Find somewhere to hide," Hunter said.

Hide? There's nowhere. Then I remembered the dead forest and the story of my salvation during the Massacre. But those lifeless woods seemed farther away than the lost city of books, where I knew we could vanish—if I could just get us there and most important, if it would let Hunter in like it had me.

"My father," I said.

We passed the door to Hunter's apartment. It opened. Rex Jones stood at the threshold, his shirt unbuttoned, his feet bare.

"What's happening?" he asked.

"P.F.R. soldiers and a Redactor," Hunter said.

I faced Rex, and like the Redactor, he saw past the open folds of my cowl at me—the real me. The connection, though brief, was damning, I knew.

I continued to our door. Hunter caught up to me. His brother barked his name.

Inside our apartment, I found my father sitting up, looking more present than I could remember in recent years. Oblivious to the danger in a way that couldn't be blamed on the F.O.G., he smiled at me.

"Pal," he said. Then he noticed Hunter and nodded. "I'm so glad you have a friend. A good friend who cares about you and will help protect you."

Hunter set his arm on my shoulder and held on. My father's smile altered, still there but now melancholy.

"You deserve to have love, Palermo. Have I told you how much I loved your mother?"

"Yes, Baba," I answered feeling trepidation, not knowing why yet.

"And how much love filled me the instant I first met you?" My father took a deep look at me. "From that moment, I knew your situ was right—you are special. The most special boy in the world."

I cupped my father's face between my hands and kissed his forehead. He deserved so much better than this life.

"I know of a place. We can go there—we'll be safe and happy," I said.

"Where?" Hunter asked from over my shoulder. "How do we get there?"

I shrugged. "I'm not sure."

"Then how do you know where it is, that it's safe?"

"Because I've been there."

I straightened and turned in search of any surface with a reflection.

"*Situ*," I called. "Help us!"

Audible through the door, originating from the hallway, came heavy footsteps and a thrum of sinister energy. The Redactor and soldiers were close. I imagined them reaching Hunter's apartment.

A succession of loud, angry knocks and the door crashing in confirmed my guess. We were next.

I spun around. The sour confines of the front room blurred. When the world again focused, I found myself staring up at the smiling sundial face whose hours seemed frozen in time. I had returned to Bibliopolis!

I turned. Hunter and my father weren't there, only the ghost of my grandmother.

"Where—?" I begged. "Where are Baba and Hunter?"

Greeting my grandmother's sad gaze, the brief flash of relief I experienced died. She shook her head.

"Why?" I demanded.

"Because now is not the time."

"I don't understand."

"You will," she said. "When the moment is right."

"The moment? That Redactor saw me—the real me! I know it did."

My grandmother nodded. "As you've come to understand more—as you've evolved—it's been harder to keep you hidden. On that terrible day, you spoke your first word and they heard you. Do you know what that word was, Palermo?"

I shrugged, the rest of my anatomy paralyzed. My brain was stuck in the fear for my beloved and my father.

"*Book*," she said. "You spoke your first word on that dark, final day."

A chill teased the nape of my neck. I fought it, failed. The shiver tumbled down my spine. "The Mother's Day Massacre—it was my fault?"

"No," she said, her sad smile gone. "The blame—the blood spilled—that stain is entirely theirs! You spoke and something in them heard what you said. Now, you've fallen in love. You're *evolving* and almost ready to fulfill your destiny, Palermo, and they've sensed that, too. You are special, my grandson. And they are damned. They know this. They want everyone to be doomed along with them. The Redactors will sacrifice all to find you and, through you, this city, and destroy Bibliopolis forever! The risk—"

"Risk? What about my father and Hunter?"

"—is too great."

The city, which had sat in silence around us, erupted with the first of a series of powerful thunderclaps—what struck my ear was a cannonade similar to the attack the P.F.R. had made across the fallen city. The courtyard trembled beneath us, the ground telegraphing the forces at work. I turned from my grandmother in time to see one of the library buildings collapse in upon itself.

No, *fold,* my inner voice corrected.

In sequence, half a dozen of the nearest structures followed suit, stone peaks and angles and friezes tucking together and sealing flat against their foundations. The tall obelisks retracted. Arches and walking paths vanished. The city was going into hiding, mimicking something I remembered from past visits spent inside the children's wing.

Closing like a popup book! I realized.

The last of the thunderclaps erupted from the giant sundial. At long last, shadows appeared across its smiling stone face, signaling a shift in time. The rays of the sun drew in like peek-a-boo fingers. The carved stone face folded over in half causing displaced hurricane winds to swirl around me. In the next instant, the massive stone envelope of the sundial came slamming down on top of me. All went dark.

"The time isn't right," my grandmother said.

The echo faded before surging back and becoming something else—fists pounding on the door!

I had returned to the front room of our hopeless apartment. A second later, the door flew open. The Redactor and its soldiers stormed in.

For a moment, I was so stunned over my brief visit to Bibliopolis and the city's collapse that I forgot to bow. The closest of the soldiers raced over, reminding me of my disrespect and any woman's role in P.F.R. society with a hard shove to the floor.

Hunter moved to protect me. "Don't touch her!"

That earned him the butt of a soldier's rifle to the vulnerable flesh of his belly. I heard all the air rush out of Hunter's lungs as he dropped, too, and the surly shuffle of the Redactor gliding closer, a slither of dust and desiccation.

"Assaulting a guard on an official P.F.R. mission is an offence punishable by death," the Redactor said in a deep, distant voice that sounded like it had originated from the bottom of a well.

The soldier flipped his weapon around and aimed the muzzle of the curse-thrower at Hunter. I stepped between them without hesitation and saw the end of my life, one more body for the fire pits, nothing particularly special about it. Not that a shot from point-blank range by the P.F.R.'s choice of assault rifle would leave much for the flames to consume. I would gladly die for Hunter. For the brief acceptance of the real me I had known with him.

Love—my grandmother had invoked the word before Bibliopolis folded in upon itself, denying us haven from the enemy. I loved Hunter, and he loved me in return. Standing between him, an insignificant young man disguised as a girl, my crimes had doubled in that one defiant act. I whispered, "No," while staring at the weapon.

It heard that one word.

"*Wait*," the Redactor bellowed.

It raised its misshapen right hand, talons extended, and aimed them at me. The horror's monocle lit. Tracer lights swept over me. I sensed the unpleasant scrutiny as whatever hybrid eyes housed in the device scanned me. I concentrated my thoughts on the floor, the dust over it, the faded concrete; trying to make those images all that this thing could find in my brain.

"It isn't fully… *exactly*… human," the Monocle said, not to the soldiers but more to itself, maybe the others of its obscene kind listening through their telepathy or the tech housed in the eye device.

"You leave my son alone," my father said.

My father, who would have been safe had I not insisted that he sever his connection to the grey F.O.G.—I had forced him to be present, and, in that one action, I had doomed my baba.

He surged off the sofa. A nod from the Redactor, and the other soldier who'd invaded our small, sad world opened fire. One blast. The center of my father's torso sprayed across the sofa and wall.

I screamed, no longer a prisoner to my terror but a slave to my rage. The Redactor towered over me, for an instant stretching up and out to the size of a T-Rex. Taller, a *kaiju* from the lost cinematic culture of a place called Japan. I didn't care if it was the height of the Colossus at Rhodes or the Statue of Liberty. I seized hold of its outstretched arm, expecting nothing more than the weft of dead leaves. But to my shock, the Redactor was solid, its hot flesh as dense as basalt, lead, or dark matter.

It tossed me aside with the ease it would a child's stuffed animal.

My father was dead.

Hunter and I were alive but existing on borrowed seconds. From the cut of my eye, I noticed movement at our open front door—Rex, still barefoot, his shirt on but unbuttoned, his head bowed, and two additional soldiers.

One of the P.F.R. guards escorting Rex broke formation and approached the Redactor.

"Eminence, he says he has information on the ones who live here," the soldier said. "In exchange for his brother's life."

The soldier pointed the muzzle of his curse-thrower down at Hunter. The Redactor harrumphed and tipped a look at Rex. All emotion ironed off Rex's face under the Monocle's notice.

"Speak," the monster commanded.

"That one, walking into the dead forest on a couple of different days. And dressed up like a girl… *he* isn't a female!"

The Redactor exhaled again, that dry, desert sound like a rustle of dead leaves and shed snakeskin. My father was gone. I'd been unmasked. What was the point of anything? Anything except saving Hunter.

Turning away from Rex and back to me, the Redactor lifted me effortlessly from the floor and held me up by my cloak.

"You are the anomaly we've searched for; the one we've known the existence of who will lead us to that hidden city of books."

I struggled against the demon's dark matter grip. Failing to force my release, I spit. The wad of my saliva struck the Redactor's monocle. The instrument again activated and caressed me with its unwanted strobes.

The Redactor turned me from side to side and examined my skull.

"Curious—no F.O.G. connector port, and yet there is something implanted in the frontal cortex of the subject's brain. Yes, I agree. Further examination is warranted."

The Redactor lowered me to my feet.

"Where is Bibliopolis? Identify location and/or coordinates," the Monocle ordered.

"I don't know," I said.

The Monocle leaned closer. A strange heat emanated off its papery flesh. In addition to all the knowledge and dreams it had absorbed, I wondered if its mutated hide radiated a powerful fever, perhaps left over from the flames. Then it drew back and tipped its focus once more to the soldiers who'd murdered my father.

"The location of The City of Books," it said.

The guard raised his curse-thrower and pressed its muzzle against Hunter's skull.

"No, please," Rex begged from across the room. His outburst earned him a shove to his knees under the threat of execution.

"I swear to you, I don't know," I said.

I inched my gaze over to Hunter's wide eyes. A deathly silence fell over the room. Waves of sickly heat pulsed off the Monocle's corpse.

The Redactor turned away and strode to the door. "Bring them both," it ordered with its back aimed our way.

One soldier muscled Hunter up from his knees and shoved him toward the door. The guard closest to me led me after them, past Rex who eyed me with a mix of rage and hatred, and back into the night. I wanted to cry out and couldn't catch my breath as they fast-marched us across the brown lawn to the troop transport. The Monocle entered ahead of us. The soldiers in their teal and charcoal uniforms with the hated Saturn symbol of the P.F.R. forced us inside. The transport stunk of years of male sweat—that of the guards and, likely, their prisoners, the Redactor, and fumes from the fuel.

They bound our wrists in thin, indestructible ties and thrust us down on one side of the miserable metal benches that lined the windows. Guards produced black hoods. My terror surged one fraction higher than its maxed-out volume.

"Not that one," the Monocle said indicating me.

They forced the hood over Hunter's head but left me to witness our final voyage into oblivion. Last second exchanges were made between pilot and platoon. The transport's engines ramped up their cacophony. The vehicle shook, rose inelegantly, paused for a second then continued its ascent. Through the windows I caught the top floors of the building where my father's body waited to be carted off to the fire pits. We crested Building Q. The transport banked, and I wondered if it would crash into the structure. But we would have no such luck.

It leveled out, flew past the closest of the Alphabet Complex prisons, and trimmed its course toward distant lights. I knew without asking where we were headed. Past the Outer Rings. Beyond even the Inner. We were on course toward the only destination possible: the Core of Saturn City, seat of power to the People's Free Republic and home of the Redactors.

Ninth Interlude

"Max?" Bernadette asked.

"Max Lencher," the strange man acknowledged during a slow wander up and down the library stacks.

"Is that your real name?" she challenged.

"Maybe. These days, people like us can't be too cautious. You've no doubt heard about the incident in Savannah."

"Their library? Of course."

"Set on fire, along with the librarians," her visitor said.

He paused long enough to invoke some of the names and titles in front of him. "*The Time Machine* by H.G. Wells. *The Last Star Warden* by Jason McCuiston. *Acadia Event* by M.J. Preston. And all of the Regency romances by Dame Barbara Cartland. It's quite the diverse and varied collection."

"It will get bigger and more complete," Bernadette said.

He looked up. "As I understand it, your goal is to curate every book ever published."

"All the ones that have survived, yes," she said before walking back the comment. "Most of them, anyway."

He flashed a knowing little smirk. "I take it you're okay with banning some of those books from your project."

"Should *Mein Kampf* and *The Art of the Deal* not make it in, I can live with it," Bernadette said dryly.

Max, or whoever he was, nodded and resumed his perusal of the titles. "Roald Dahl, Zane Grey, Tolkien…" He picked up the top book from a pile. "*The Emperor's Guard* by Kevin Hopson. George R.R. Martin. Robert E. Howard. Very thorough, Bernadette."

"It's Mrs. Bistany to you," she fired back.

Max flashed a tired smile. "Of course. Forgive me for assuming we'd reached the point of first name basis."

"I don't know your name."

Max set down the book. "What's in a name? Ah, yes. Mine might be Max. But I am not a spy for the enemy within—those self-glorifying patriots who have no clue as to just how unpatriotic their actions really are. Their desires and end results are, in fact, the opposite. You and I have more in common than you think."

Bernadette pondered his claim. Did Max fondly remember a grandmother whose heart was shattered and was isolated and ignored by a clueless husband? Had Max nearly been murdered on the bank of the Spigot River? Was Max's son presently in mourning for a child that would never draw breath let alone read Lewis Carroll or Jane Yolen?

"What you're attempting here—and succeeding mightily at," Max continued, clarifying their similarities, "is also being initiated elsewhere. Not just literature but our art, languages, our music, and the celluloid culture, which are all in jeopardy of being erased. *Incinerated*."

"How do you know about my project?"

Again, that secretive smile. "I work in tech. Okay, you could say that I *am* tech."

You look like you live in your car, she thought but resisted voicing the comeback.

"My company has made a lot of money in the field of new technologies—and upgrading old ones with quantum leaps forward in design and effectiveness."

Then Max moved aside some of the scraggly wisps of his hair and tilted his head, just so, to reveal another of the night's surprises. At first, Bernadette wasn't sure what she was looking at.

"Yes, it's a data port," Max said right as she made the connection. "Meaning that I can plug in and experience the data like a living computer. Oh, I know what you're thinking—" He lowered the lock of grey hair and waved a hand with theatrical flourish.

Know what I'm thinking? That the person standing near King, Shirley Jackson, and Richard Matheson is a madman?

"—that I'm some cyborg come from the future, here to terminate you." Max laughed. "That one never gets old."

Bernadette exhaled. "That's where you're wrong."

The levity evaporated from Max's expression. "Okay, so I was an experiment—a vanguard, if you will. First one. Couldn't expect anybody else to boldly go where I, myself, was unwilling to. That was a while ago. Like I said, things have improved. Very much so."

The deep hurt churning in Bernadette's stomach sharpened. Her thoughts returned to the hospital room; the despair and the widening shadows that now shrouded her wherever she turned.

"Your plan is noble, but it's also doomed," he said.

Her walls were back up. "Oh?"

"For a number of reasons—the first being logistics. Where do you plan to store so many books?"

There it was again, that one vital flaw in her plan whose solution eluded her.

"In my house if I have to," she answered, her tone defiant.

"And there's the next reason—you'd be giving these zealots two easy targets. With just two raids they could destroy it all."

Max picked up a hardcover off the shelf and examined it. Bernadette knew the volume's identity—the collected works of Anton Chekov. That same grouping contained a Who's Who of the greatest playwrights in history including Tennessee Williams, Arthur Miller, Ibsen, O'Neil, and Mamet.

"Without the words, all of this is only paper. To house so many books would require a city—and as we've seen, cities burn just like paper."

The shadow around her darkened. Why bother when all this was for nothing? For a starling instant, she recalled her late situ sitting slumped in a chair, marinating in sweat, and having mostly surrendered.

Why bother?! For dandelion greens, grape leaves, and a magical day at the library surrounded by books. For Lebanon. For Haley's Comet. For the matter of souls.

"Tell me," she said, hoping his answer would dispel the encroaching gloom like a fan would the humidity. "Tell me how we can build a safe city."

Max reached into his pocket and pulled out a tiny device. "With this. I told you we'd upgraded old tech to the point it is now superior—like going from the stone wheel to the space station. And we're working on even greater storage capacity as we download, curate, and protect in preparation for what is coming."

He tossed the thumb drive to her. Bernadette caught it.

"And what's next?" she asked.

"Details. The destination—we're still on the journey. But the journey is being fast-tracked by those aggressive murderers."

She listened, nodded. "Are you suggesting an alliance?"

"Yes. You're the kind of soul I want to work with. The kind who will save our future from these criminal assholes. Which leads me to the next salient point."

Max put down the Chekov book and stepped closer.

"The system—this library. This *city* of books," he gestured around the whole room. "Once we have the destination, the defense system, it will need a librarian. I can think of no other more ideal candidate than you, Bernadette."

* * *

Months passed.

Books burned.

Cities, too.

What had started overseas had ignited on home soil, leading to emergency sessions of congress, marshal law, and the suspension of the old rules, codes, and ideals that had steered the country's course for centuries. All that vanished in just months.

On one of the last days of that old world, Bernadette entered the bedroom, a babe clutched in her hands. The family huddled in the darkness. The power had been cut. With it, all news from the outside world went dark. But you didn't need TV, phones, or the internet to hear the assaults taking place outside as families were rounded up for relocation to the new construction project far from all that was familiar.

"Ted, Lawrence," she said in a voice barely louder than a whisper. "*Diane.*"

They looked up. The babe kicked, proof of life even as death closed in around them.

From somewhere close enough to be heard, a detonation boomed.

"Ma?" Lawrence asked.

She faced them, her beautiful daughter-in-law, broken over the loss of a child like her situ in that other life and time; her son, who was a good man, a hard worker, and would become a great father; and, finally, Ted, who had given those same qualities to their son. Ted, who she loved and always would.

Bernadette handed over the baby to Lawrence, who took him into a gentle and protective fold.

Diane seemed to come back to life. "A son?"

"Your son. All of our sons. His name is Palermo," Bernadette said.

"*Palermo*," Diane said, speaking the baby's name like a sweet incantation.

"Hey, Pal," said Lawrence.

He handed the baby to Diane. She held Palermo. Tears spilled down her cheeks. As Ted drew Bernadette close and the madness of angry fists pounded at their front door, the baby's eyes met Bernadette's. A look of silent understanding passed between them, and she heard Max's voice. Max, who was gone, dead, and all else that he'd built and achieved either destroyed or corrupted in the hands of those criminals who were now calling themselves the People's Free Republic.

You'll be the perfect librarian, he said in her memory.

Librarian? she questioned.

Or, to be specific, the perfect A.I. to guard over Bibliopolis and the Protective Autonomic Library-Encoded Retrieval Mobile Organism.

PALERMO

Palermo!

"I love him," the boy's new mother said.

Love. That and the dimming light of hope for a future that looked already gone were all that was left. Bernadette closed her eyes for the time it took to pray for mercy to whatever deity was listening.

None was.

Armed P.F.R. soldiers in their new teal and charcoal uniform colors with the hateful symbol of a circle encased in a ring kicked in the door.

And the new Dark Age of Humanity officially began.

Chapter

Ten

I pressed as close to Hunter as possible. "I love you," I said. Hunter sat with his hooded head bowed, and I chastised myself for thinking he looked like one about to be executed. He was.

"I'm so sorry, Palermo," Hunter said, his voice reaching me above the roar of the transport's turbines. "I love you, too."

The unpleasant slither of an unwanted gaze drew my focus up to its source: the Redactor. Its monocled eye was lit and trained upon me.

"What are you?" it asked.

"My father's son," I said. "One more of your victims."

"We'll see what is so different about you once we reach the cathedral."

It had no real mouth, when closed it was only a cyan flecked stain where one had been long before, but I swore the killer of my father smiled.

"Cathedral?" I asked. "You do think highly of yourselves. You Redactors are no gods."

The Monocle leaned back and crossed one bony leg over the other in a pose that might have looked comical if not for its macabre presentation. "That's where you are wrong. Gods create in their images. Look around you."

I shot a glance at the soldiers, all subservient, all worshippers wearing the colors and symbol of false gods. Past the window glass at the glow of Saturn City, so named for its rings of ever increasing poverty. Ahead and below us, it was lit up brightly against the new night. Identifiers flashed red from a line of multi-limbed broadcasting towers—the source of the F.O.G. signal. The entrance to Hell, a version more terrible than Dante or Blatty ever envisioned in their most famous literary works.

"You destroyed the world," I said.

"Be silent, you disrespectful—" the nearest of the guards barked.

The Monocle held up its taloned hand. "No, let it speak. It amuses me."

"*Murderer*," I spat.

"*God*," the Redactor said. "Creator of Heaven and Earth. I am immortal. There is no power greater than mine!"

I turned away, denying the fake god of this world further attention. The Core of Saturn City loomed beyond the windows, a center of tall buildings that scraped the dark sky.

At their center was a grey, malevolent structure connected by metal thorns to thick conduit that pulsed with a sallow glow. Giant flags bearing the circle and ring symbol waved in the polluted breeze. Without it being explained to me, I knew that place was the cathedral.

The transport descended.

The execution commenced.

* * *

They marched us out of the craft and along a tarmac. I could only guess of the multitudes of other souls who'd been forced along this same route toward the thorned complex soaking up endless grey energy from the F.O.G. towers.

The air thrummed with an undercurrent that rippled over my flesh, vibrated in my molars, my marrow.

Deeper, in what I sometimes thought of as soul, my terror surged. My father's face appeared between the shutter-clicks of blinks.

"*Pal*," he said.

Then I saw the canvas of the wall behind the sofa red with his blood. Words appeared. I attempted to guide the narration. That failed, and the words damned me.

Abandon all hope, ye who enter here, they read.

Through the colorless courtyard where an eternal flame burned, a reminder of the fires the Redactors had scorched the planet with to reshape it in its present image of desolation.

Through the cathedral's double doors which bore the hated symbol of their regime and opened with a jarring creak, releasing a toxic teal glow that illuminated walls, floor, and ceiling.

Through the acre of conduit that ran like the pipes of an organ—an instrument that only played funeral dirges.

To the doors that led into their sadistic worship hall.

"Remove that one to the processing area—and make sure to connect it to the F.O.G.," the Monocle ordered.

Two of the soldiers strong-armed Hunter away and down a corridor located between the conduits.

"No," I protested.

The Redactor grabbed me by the back of my cloak and dragged me through those doors. No P.F.R. soldiers followed us.

The music of death stung at my ears and drilled into my brain. All around me was a scene from the worst nightmare ever dreamed. What I guessed to be a hundred Redactors or more sat on thrones in a crescent, each of the horrors dressed in dusty black and white suits. All were plugged into the network of F.O.G. cables descending from the cavernous ceiling like grey umbilical cords, each tentacle feeding stolen life into the husks that thought themselves gods.

The Monocle forced me onto a patch of floor directly in front of the crescent of desiccated corpses.

"What is it?" one voice asked.

"The source of the signal we detected?" another posed.

"I believe so," the Monocle said.

My captor reached down, seized my cloak in both of its skeleton hands, and tore the heavy fabric apart with the ease of ripping through tissue. I spilled naked at its feet.

"A male? Disguised as a female?" another of the voices bellowed. "To avoid detection. To hide among them unseen."

"It has no connection port," the Monocle reported.

* * *

Pain exploded along the right side of my skull as the teeth of the instrument drilled through scalp, blood vessels, and, finally, bone. The twisting caught my hair and ripped chunks of it out while driving other bits of hair deep into the wound. The same Redactor performing the surgery without anesthetic held me down with its other hand, the strength of that act nearly as painful as the implant procedure.

My misery deepened at a crunching sound, signaling bone had been fully breached. I begged my own consciousness to wink out. It didn't, leaving me out of body, an observer to the horror. My mind recorded the hunger of those metal teeth. Having chewed their way into my skull, they stilled. The device's maw widened and it spit venom in the form of circuitry and connections. As soon as the data port was inside me, I sensed the feelers latching onto my grey matter.

The Monocle observed its fellow Redactor's progress, its mechanical eye lit. "Insertion complete. Unit ready for activation," it reported.

"And that other implant?" the Butcher asked.

"Still inert."

The horror holding me down on the metal surgical table reached up. A grey F.O.G. cable snaked down from the overhead apparatus and it plugged the connection into my new port, linking me to the network sipping and sucking the life out of everyone.

At first, the pain from being butchered while awake dulled the sensory blast of the connection.

"The anomaly?" the Butcher asked.

The Monocle scanned me. "No change. If we don't learn what we seek through the F.O.G., we will remove it from the subject's brain for analysis."

"Removal will kill the subject."

"So be it," the Monocle said.

* * *

The greyness crept up on me like wispy haze in an old Gothic novel. I was aware of the operating theater, the two monsters within its sinister walls, and of my agony, pulsing red-hot in exquisite waves from the site of the implant.

The fog rolled in. I saw my captors loom over me, monsters from a waking nightmare. A kind of fever took possession of all conscious thought. My senses blurred. I stared into the shadowiness and narrowed my inner eye. Within the mist, I made out tiny electric flashes. *Stars*, I thought. Then it struck me that I was seeing the pulses of a brain. Each of the stars emitted a kind of music.

A dirge.

They were the bursts of energy and life being robbed from the people linked into the network.

Frozen, I stared harder. I don't know when I woke enough to wonder if I could communicate with the other minds out there trapped in the fog. But as soon as I did, I again grew conscious of my captors—not just the two in the surgical room but of the hundred more in the cathedral's obscene worship hall, all plugged in and feasting on stolen life energy.

"It is still aware," one of those false gods said in an alien baritone.

"Impossible. The F.O.G. should cancel out all individuality," the Butcher answered. "Is it the anomalous device?"

The Monocle answered, "Still no change in readings. The subject hears us."

"Impossible!"

But I did hear them. I stared into the flashes. So many stars. A million constellations. If afterlives existed beyond this veil of tears, I prayed in silence that my baba had gone to the best possible. That he was reunited with my mother, his father, and my situ.

"*Situ?*" the Butcher asked.

And how I sent back my hatred to it, to all of the Redactors. *You don't get to speak that holy word, most vile demons!*

"Subject is not feeding life force into the F.O.G.," said the Monocle. "Checking connection and implanted data port."

More pain exploded through me, only this time I welcomed it. The greyness thinned.

"Immunity?" one voice posed.

"Also impossible. There are no prior recorded examples of immunity among humans."

"As you have already determined, the subject isn't entirely human."

Bleeding, conscious of everything happening around and inside my mind, I focused on the constellations.

Sirius—in the constellation Canis Major, I thought. *Hunter, do you hear me?*

An image flashed before my mind's eye of Hunter, still cuffed, beaten, lying in a painful fetal curl on the floor of a holding cell, attached to a F.O.G. cable snaking down from the ceiling.

"Palermo?" he whispered in response, both from his split and bloodied lip in the real world and somewhere in the constellation Canis Major. "Where are you?"

"Speak to me—I'll follow your voice," I said.

His mouth moved. Fragments of words spilled forth along with those he was thinking which filled in gaps.

"…remembering how beautiful you were. Even more so when I saw the real you. You gave me a reason to hope for something better. Some place far away, like the moon. "

I focused on the lights. One eight-pointed, tiny golden star grew brighter as though in the throes of a super nova.

"*Hunter*," I called.

He stepped out of the light and into my arms. I again recorded Hunter's magnificence—that handsome face with its scruff, those blue eyes, and his incredible physique. More attractive than any of it was the aura that lingered around him, his effulgence proof of love and something more, something greater.

Maybe it wasn't only life that the Redactors devoured from their victims but also soul.

"It's listening to us," the Butcher said.

"Then hear this, human—if you do not divulge the exact coordinates of the City of Books, this human you profess to love will be executed."

I looked around. The greyness was back, superimposed everywhere. Gazing up into Hunter's eyes, I saw my grandmother reflected in the blue of his pupils. She nodded. I didn't question her order.

"Prepare to receive coordinates," I said.

Hunter's grip on me tightened.

I held on and betrayed the location of Bibliopolis.

* * *

A familiar coolness embraced me, a second hug that complimented Hunter's. Still holding onto him, I blinked. He was here, with me, and we had traveled the distance of light years to Bibliopolis. We stood in one of the grand wings where wooden columns capped in carved acanthus leaves and rolling ladders soared up between shelves of books stacked twenty high.

Hunter gasped. "Where are we?"

Relief washed over me. It had worked! We were here. "Safe, Hunter."

He released me but only partway. Hunter glanced around us. "What—?"

"Books. Literature. Every story and fact ever written down throughout all of history," I said.

Eyes wide, he drank in the world of words.

"We're in Bibliopolis, it's the lost city of books," I said.

I took his hand and led him over to the nearest window. Outside, the central courtyard spread before us. The city had unfolded and, once more, the giant sundial face smiled.

"I don't understand," Hunter said. "A second ago, I was in a prison cell."

I tipped a look at his face. Hunter's lips weren't split open and clotting with blood over cheap blows by one or more P.F.R. guards.

"Something's wrong," I said. "And the last time I was here, the city sealed in upon itself, like it was going into hiding… like a book's cover closing."

Hunter touched his lips and examined his fingers. I reached toward my head. Searing agony erupted from the place where my skull had been punctured and the F.O.G. implant forced upon my grey matter. Hunter caught me as I started to topple.

"Palermo?"

I steadied. "I'm still attached to the F.O.G. cable. I don't understand what's happening. Why—?"

A jagged sound sliced through the otherworldly calm of Bibliopolis. I tracked it past the window and outside the library building's wall to a patch of placid blue sky above the sundial's face in time to see a shadow descend over the clock's smile.

A P.F.R. transport swooped down and landed at the heart of the courtyard. The transport's engine belched dirty brown smoke across the pristine space, obscuring our view as a dozen dark shapes strode out, taking in their surroundings with a different kind of interest.

The smoke thinned. One of the Redactors looked up at the window where Hunter and I stood. It activated the monocle device anchored to the dark stain where an eye once was. The Monocle faced me. My insides froze.

The other Redactors took formation behind the Monocle. Time stopped. The universe held its breath.

Then the Monocle raised its taloned hand, and the Redactors surged forward. Time unstuck. The world exhaled. Doors banged open with such force that I heard glass shatter and frames crack.

The Redactors had located Bibliopolis. I had betrayed the city along with all of the words ever written throughout human history. On my grandmother's signal, I had redacted the last hope for the future.

"What do we do, Palermo?" Hunter asked.

"I'll tell you what we do," said a voice from behind, a young girl's.

We both whirled to see her, a moppet of maybe twelve with dark hair and a beauty mark.

"*We fight!*" she said.

I blinked, and standing where the girl had been was Bernadette Bistany, my grandmother.

Tenth Interlude

"This is how we fight," she recalled Max saying. "This is how we stop them!" Pain shattered the vision. Max, railing against the brutal new regime and its growing list of atrocities, vanished in a wash of crimson before Bernadette's eyes. She recorded the acrid puff of smoke from the teeth of the drill as it connected with skull bone, the crunch, and the sensory rush when her brain was briefly exposed to air in the fractured second before the data port was implanted.

In that sliver of time, she recalled clearly Einstein's formula for the black hole. With it came the ending of Poe's famous poem *Lenore*—a favorite she'd memorized as a girl working at the library to replace destroyed books, along with dramatic memories from a soap opera she'd followed in her teens and twenties, passages from the novel *Peyton Place*, and the hypnotic swirls of Vincent Van Gough's *The Starry Night* painting. For a startling instant, she found herself traveling up through the galactic wastelands between star systems, her body flying with arms extended toward the effulgence of a distant star—Sirius or Alpha Centauri or Vega.

The instant passed, and the agony caught up.

Bernadette howled. She attempted to hold onto the last of all that remained good. The P.A.L.E.R.M.O. unit had been delivered safely, the last and most vital part of Max's technological genius. Max was gone, his earlier creations blasphemed by the enemy. The searing pain drilled into her brain, forced upon her and everyone else against their wills. The world had been set aflame like the Great Library at Alexandria. But all wasn't lost. No, they had succeeded even as they'd failed.

Not all had been incinerated.

Bernadette forgot that in the surge of nothingness that slammed into her as the P.F.R. butcher who'd performed the violation connected her to the cable, and her head filled with grey fog. Something about the ones who'd set the fires... they'd changed and were no longer technically human. They'd burned the books and had, themselves, been burned. They'd inhaled the ashes, swallowed the flames. She'd seen one of them while the soldiers went from house to house and rounded up families and survivors, forcing the F.O.G. upon them. It looked like Nosferatu with its facial features eroded, burned away, its skin like old paper, its clothes exuding a stink of bonfires and char.

Redactors, she thought, attempting to hold onto the word. Only it, too, shattered into dust and everything around and inside her went grey in the billows of nothingness waiting on the other side of the end of the war.

* * *

Bernadette dressed in the miserable garb assigned to women. In this new order, she was nobody, invisible. The very notion conjured rage in her belly. But she knew her grandson needed to be protected, and invisibility wasn't without benefits.

She faced her reflection in the mirror above the dresser. The miserable beige walls of the apartment they'd been relocated to stared back along with the cloaked woman who'd once survived an attempted murder at the hands of another monster.

"I will survive this, too," she whispered.

She broke focus with the mirror and passed the other bedroom. Lawrence was sprawled face down on the bed, attached to the wall cable and lost in the grey noise being pumped through wires and into brains. She found Ted in the living room, similarly hooked into the F.O.G. Ted rarely spoke now and was almost not there. The same sinking hopelessness gripped her as she remembered the body wagons and removal teams of undertakers that seemed to visit the complex and its alphabetized buildings daily. No one spoke about the ground pits smoking past the tree line of the dying forest, but everyone could smell the charnel stink in the air and knew what they were doing. The ash from all the culture, all the books and pictures, burned in the Redactions still fell from the sky, and the remains of names and lives already forgotten were being added to the four winds for unceremonious scattering.

Diane and her son sat in a dirty, castoff recliner salvaged from a pile left at the curb along with other refuse from homes no longer there. Though not plugged into the F.O.G., Diane looked barely present. Bernadette spoke her name. Diane returned from the greyness. Palermo kicked his legs.

"I think something's wrong with him," the cloaked zombie said.

"Wrong?" Bernadette asked.

"He doesn't cry, doesn't speak."

"He will. And maybe he doesn't cry because he's happy."

It was an insane thing to say, and Diane called her out on it. *"Happy?"*

All right, not happy but busy, Bernadette thought. *Busy hearing all about knights and castles, bases on the moon and first contact encounters with alien races. He's sailing oceans, learning to translate*

English into foreign languages, and studying ancient cultures. He's preparing for the future… readying to lead us out of this very dark time.

"There's nothing wrong with your son," Bernadette said. "We have to protect him. He's special. He's the future."

Diane cradled the baby. Bernadette kissed both of their foreheads. The food delivery was due soon. *Food*—that was a generous term for the unpalatable and unhealthy slop being processed at the P.F.R. packing plants far from the Outer Rings of the Alphabet Complex. Her mind traveled back in time to meals of stuffed grape leaves and fluffy eggs filled with diced, sautéed dandelion greens and a tear invaded the corner of her eye. She willed the deluge back behind her armor and barely succeeded.

"He needs to remain hidden," Bernadette said.

"How?" Diane asked.

The question challenged her, because Bernadette didn't know the answer. "Hidden," she repeated, aware of the heaviness of the hated cloak that made her invisible. With her next labored breath, she had the solution.

* * *

She walked along the sidewalk, mostly invisible. Above her, the sky drifted with gauzy grey clouds that could have been heavy with rain but were, more likely, filled with ash. Ahead of her, Building D rose up, that last stop on her daily walk before Bernadette turned around to return to the hopeless apartment they'd been damned to inhabit in C.

Her library was gone. Daisy Street seemed part of a dream now, a place as foggy as the one that slithered out of the cable, calling to her and everyone else to plug into it with a hypnotic siren's song. The only thing of value that remained was family.

I'll protect them, she thought.

At Building D, the corpse wagon sat parked near the entrance. Another body for the flames.

Another book, her inner voice said. *We're all our own unique stories, and they have stolen the words and set the pages on fire.*

* * *

Not long after making that promise, she found Ted in the curbside-rescued chair, his lips blue, his skin grey. He was still connected to the F.O.G. cable.

Bernadette wailed for six days, convinced her eyes would shrivel after releasing an endless cascade of tears. The corpse wagon arrived as though, somehow, the ones who removed the bodies for burning knew that a life had expired. Her lover, her husband, her partner, was gone forever.

The F.O.G., she thought when Bernadette could reason again after the loss. *They aren't only pumping grey noise into the minds of everyone connected to the data port—they're listening. Worse, they're taking something from us!*

With Ted gone, she stopped eating. A lack of appetite was easy to attain given what the P.F.R. provided them. Bernadette slept in the bed, on her spine, with her fingers steepled. On a day no different than the one that preceded it, she realized she'd taken on a funereal pose. The corpse she had become still breathed, but the analogy was fitting. Despair had crippled her.

A thick silence hung over the apartment. Lawrence, too, was crushed by his father's death, only he'd taken to losing himself in the grey F.O.G. It dulled all emotion then sucked out energy like a leach numbing a wound and growing fat on its host's blood.

Diane had the baby, now swaddled in the disguise of all females. The notion disgusted her, but Bernadette couldn't give any energy to her anger. Ted's death had broken her.

"*Bernadette*," Diane called.

The corpse unsteepled her fingers and sat up. The room performed a spin as gravity attempted to crush her. She slipped off the bed, aware of her age and the aches in her bones in a way she'd never accepted before. Focusing, Bernadette made it from the bedroom to the front room.

"Lawrence," Diane said. She attempted to wake him from the greyness, but Lawrence was deep in the F.O.G. and beyond hearing her.

"What's wrong?" Bernadette asked.

Diane turned. She dandled Palermo, who flashed an innocent smile at the sight of his grandmother.

"Not wrong—he spoke!" Diane said.

Some of the misery lifted from Bernadette's shoulders. Like the baby, grandmother smiled. "What did he say?"

Diane cradled Palermo. "Tell her, Pal. Tell your situ what you told me!'"

Palermo giggled, blew a raspberry, and then said the unexpected, magical word: "*Book.*"

The gloom that had possessed Bernadette crumbled. The faintest glimmer of hope drew her back from the precipice. It was enough, even in its cruel brevity.

* * *

The air thundered and the apartment building shook from the vibrations of the manmade storm sweeping in on an otherwise calm May Sunday morning. The troop transports totaled a dozen before

Bernadette stopped counting. Armed P.F.R. soldiers dressed in teal and charcoal, their uniforms boasting that hated symbol, streamed out, fell in line, and waited. Bernadette's heart resumed its gallop. There was no reason to hope left. She knew the day's outcome was bleak. And that it would be her last.

From the edge of the window, she watched an abomination stride out from the last of the transports, an obscenity dressed in a faded black suit that stood an easy foot taller than the tallest man she'd ever met. Its skin looked like old paper—sallow, something shed by a snake. Where people had eyes, noses, ears, and mouths, its face bore deep cyan stains. The nightmare marching in front of the soldiers wore a device over one eye that lit fluorescent white—a high-tech version of a lens of some sort. The obscenity addressed the soldiers.

"You know what your objective is," it said in a guttural baritone, its voice the sound of a desiccated throat that had inhaled great quantities of smoke and ashes.

And, as the soldiers split into teams to carry out their horrific mission on that dark day, the Monocle turned, and Bernadette knew, somehow knew, that it was looking directly at her.

* * *

They were forced crying, screaming, out of the Alphabet Complex along with all the girls and women from the three surrounding buildings.

"What did I do?" begged one woman suddenly made visible to the soldiers. "I haven't—"

The woman received a hard shove from the nearest of the murderers herding all of them, dozens more of the innocent, toward the dying forest where few of the trees sported any spring foliage. Rage was back in Bernadette's stomach, but now instead of fueling her resolve she felt it consuming her. The fire that had already feasted on so many stories wasn't satisfied. Soon, it would consume not only her tale but also the legends of all the women and young girls being driven to their deaths.

"Why—?" another woman shrieked.

A soldier fired his curse-thrower, and the woman's head vanished from her shoulders. Blood sprayed trunks and others of the condemned; a preview of their own deaths. Chaos briefly ensued. More weapon's fire thundered through the dying forest.

At Bernadette's side, Diane opened her mouth, but no sound emerged. An instant of silent understanding passed between them. She handed Bernadette the babe disguised as a girl and, making the decision, passed Palermo's future into his grandmother's care.

Bullets sprayed the crowd of women. Bodies dropped.

Diane raised her hands, located her voice, and screamed in defiance.

Thunder pounded at Bernadette's back as she raced into the woods, the baby in her arms. *I want to fight,* she thought, holding tears back, the horror threatening to paralyze her. *I want to fight them and not stop until—*

The tree was dead, its bark shredded away, its interior opened like a cave. She dug in her soles, lowered, and met the child's terrified eyes.

"You are special," she said. "Protect Bibliopolis… and save the future! I will be with you always, I promise, my wonderful *hafid*. I love you, my grandson."

The baby's face scrunched. Palermo readied to cry. Bernadette held a finger to her lips, urging silence. The babe quieted. More thunder sounded. She whirled, facing a P.F.R. soldier standing among the dead trees, curse-thrower raised.

Bernadette froze. Then, hands balled into fists, she ran at him, screaming in a warrior woman's battle-voice.

He fired, and the world went dark.

* * *

Lawrence unplugged from the F.O.G. and returned to a foreboding silence.

"Ma," he called. "Diane?"

Nobody answered.

He stood, shaky at first, and moved around the apartment. In his mother's room, he found the mirror toppled onto the floor, the glass cracked. It was the first proof that the wrongness he sensed was real.

Men sobbed and collapsed on the scraggly lawn across the surrounding building fronts. Lawrence staggered toward a gathering of strangers who could have been neighbors—it was difficult to know anymore given the new reclusive nature of life in the Outer Rings.

"My wife, my mother," he said. "My *daughter*! Where were they taken?"

The confusion he suffered more frequently now crowded Lawrence's mind in a thick haze. He caught words, gestures. Little of it registered.

"They were looking for something," one of the possible neighbors said.

Another pointed around the building.

"They're gone. All gone," the man added.

Coldness washed through Lawrence's insides. He walked, continuing to stagger, still confused and disoriented, away from the small crowd of mourners. By the time he reached the corner of the building, he was running.

There were no bodies—those had been removed to the fire pits—only plenty of blood. Its tang hung sickening and sweet in the air, smelling of fruit that had gone past its prime and was rotting. Blood was the only fruit those dying trees would produce.

Lawrence wandered the misty, dying woods. The air stung at his throat and burned in his nostrils. Not mist, the wisps of grey were smoke made bitter from the stench of burning flesh.

"No," he moaned.

But the proof was everywhere he looked, sprayed on the trunks and across the trampled ground. He gazed up. Smoke drifted over his head, welcoming an early, artificial dusk. He wanted to cry but couldn't. All was lost. Tears, even if they were possible, wouldn't bring back the dead.

A leaf detached from a branch and made a slow descent. Brown around the edges, it drifted to the bloodstained ground, the final proof that everything good was gone.

Lawrence turned in the direction of the smoke. The fire—he'd walk right into the pit, become one more body, one more death on this day of massacres. He marched with his eyes aimed straight ahead, his steps robotic, his life ended.

Trees passed by in a slow blur, all of them dead or dying. The bitter smoke thickened inside his chest. A grey whine buzzed in his ear, his thoughts—the residual nothingness of the F.O.G. device. Lately, it was the only thing he truly cared about. So much so, he'd been in its thrall when the murderers took his wife, mother, and baby.

"*Pal*," he sobbed.

Palermo cried out to him, a wraith from the World of the Dead that would haunt these dying woods for whatever remained of eternity. Perhaps, Lawrence would join him and all the other souls damned to roam the place where they'd been slaughtered. Maybe—

The babe cried again, this time loud enough to cut through the greyness inside his skull. Lawrence halted. The next few seconds passed with a terrible heaviness as he listened, waited.

Another whimper reached his ear. It came from the surrounding trees. Lawrence tracked it to the remains of an oak. In a small cave nestled at the base, a tiny figure had been hidden. A trick of the mind? Worse, the F.O.G.?

Palermo, who never cried, mewled again, shocking Lawrence out of his confusion. He leaned down, scooped the child in his unsteady hands, and drew the boy out of hiding. Palermo shrieked. Lawrence hugged the babe.

"It's okay, Pal. Baba is here," Lawrence said.

He soothed the child, drank in the sour smell of the dying Earth and the babe's soiled clothes, and remembered how to cry. They wept together at the foot of the dying oak tree and, after a while, Lawrence carried his son out of the lifeless forest and back to the apartment where others once lived but now were gone.

CHAPTER

ELEVEN

Palermo called out. "Situ!"

Grandmother Bernadette altered form again, becoming the little girl. "I am the Librarian—the artificial intelligence assigned to guide you and watch over this construct." Then the little girl shifted shape back to my grandmother's recognizable form. "But yes, Palermo, I am your situ and everything she was."

We embraced, and how solid and warm she seemed in my arms. The fragrance of her perfume, the strength in my grandmother's hug, all of the details felt so true.

"Construct?" Hunter said. "This place isn't real?"

"It's real, Hunter," she said. "It is everything we ever were, all we can become again."

"But the Redactors," I asked. "How do we fight them? There must be a dozen of them and only three of us!"

My situ smiled, that spare grin inspiring a shiver in my soul. "Three of us, yes—but we aren't alone. Oh, no, grandson. Because of your actions—and your father's sacrifice—we are now in a unique position to strike back, *to fight!*"

The double doors behind us shattered inward. The Monocle stood at the threshold flanked by a dozen Redactors.

"Long last, Bibliopolis falls!" the Monocle said. "Take them—and destroy this place of books!"

The Redactors split, half of their number moving toward us, the rest arching their spines, craning their long necks, and peeling back the sealed, scabbed-over flesh of their mouths. From their bellies, they vomited up the embers long ago ingested during the Redactions. Flames ignited and engulfed shelves. Books caught fire. The rare volumes burned.

"Situ," I called above the horrifying music of the conflagration.

"Run, now!" she said pointing the way.

We ran, and the Monocle and his murderers pursued.

* * *

We raced down a soaring marble staircase and into another wing, this one containing scrolls and delicate, ancient papers archived within glass cases. From there, we passed into a long room filled with paperbacks and pulp magazines. At our backs, the heavy clomp of footsteps across marble echoed like tribal drumbeats announcing war. Our enemy was close.

Halfway across the room, my grandmother stopped. Hunter and I jammed behind her. She turned. At the entrance, the Monocle and its brethren caught up. White glare casting from its ocular device scanned us.

"Your library burns," the Monocle said, stalking nearer. "Your location has been targeted. You—"

"—talk too much!" my grandmother shouted.

She swung her hand through empty air. A paperback novel spilled from the nearest shelf and landed on the floor, creating a muffled thunderclap. The Monocle tipped its focus down. An instant later, a giant hand, sallow-skinned, its wrist scarred in jagged stitch marks, reached up from the book and seized hold of the Monocle's throat. Victor Frankenstein's creation stepped out of the pages and shoved the Redactor into another set of shelves, which toppled over, spilling more paperbacks across the library's floor.

And then it happened, something so unexpected and glorious in its pageantry that I briefly forgot the flames consuming other sections of the city.

Peter Benchley's great white shark erupted from the pages of the spilled mess on the floor, expanding to its full length. The beast bit down on the Butcher. An inhuman shriek carried above the cacophony of a hundred things happening at the same time.

A raven appeared, flapped its powerful wings, and attacked another of the enemy, gouging and pecking at its face while declaring, "Nevermore!"

Count Dracula joined the battle, along with Morlocks, gladiators, cowboys from the old American West, machine gun-toting suits, and Martians armed with death rays. An army of literature's greatest monsters and villains had risen as heroes against the Redactors.

The Monocle thrust Frankenstein back and activated its ocular device. "Send in reinforcements! I repeat, all are needed to redact Bibliopolis!"

My grandmother gripped my hand and took Hunter's in her other. "Hurry! They are just buying us a little time, they can't hold them for long."

We resumed running.

"But what about the city—the *books*?" I called above the sounds of battle.

"It isn't time," she said.

We burst into another wing where the Redactors had already set the collections on fire. My grandmother pivoted toward a corridor. A single door marked its ending point. We ran through and emerged onto the courtyard beneath the sundial's face. That location allowed us to see the devastation taking place around us. Bibliopolis burned. Each second meant more history and literature was lost.

The sky over our heads, already filled with oily black smoke, trembled under the onslaught of something far worse. Ten more P.F.R. troop transports streaked down from the horizon and landed around the courtyard. I cast a look at the sundial face, smiling even as Bibliopolis fell and more Redactors joined the slaughter, its expression frozen in time.

Time.

I blinked, and it was my face staring down from the vast stone edifice. A strange, cool energy surged through my insides.

"Yes, Palermo—at long last, *it's time,*" the little girl version of my grandmother said, turning me away from my reflection on the sundial. "The last of them is here!"

For another moment, the city was an inferno. Redactors spilled out of their transports, dozens of them, every last murderer of innocents, literature, and history. The Monocle strode out of the smoke, the char of burned pages wafting off its clothes and skin.

"This is the end," it said.

"Yes," I said. "An ending for you—and a new beginning for the world!"

Without the words, books are only paper, I thought. Closing my eyes, I willed the illusion to end and the truth to surface. A shadow appeared on the sundial, signaling one tick of the clock forward. In that second, the fires cut out across the city. Bibliopolis stood whole, her collections restored. I faced the enemy. There would be no more running from them.

"Impossible!" the Monocle growled.

A hundred other Reactors lined up behind it, every last one of those soulless murderers. All of them. Focused on me.

"We are all our own stories," I said, holding the hand of the little girl who was once my grandmother on my left, Hunter's on my right. "You have stolen those narratives. It is time you returned them."

"This city—!" the Monocle attempted.

"Is *me*. I am Bibliopolis, and your time is over!"

I shut my eyes and imagined a great book closing, sealing together. Around me, the Redactors cried out, but their inhuman peals waned and the echo died. Bibliopolis, a city of books and wisdom, blurred around me. I woke on the surgical table, naked and bleeding and still connected to the F.O.G. cable.

A strangulated, guttural wheeze drifted through the haze, anchoring me back to my place in the cathedral of false gods. The room surfaced from the greyness just in time for me to see two sets of empty black suits and white shirts crumple to the floor, each releasing a small cloud of smoke upon impact. Elsewhere in the worship hall, through a kind of false telepathy that could have been the F.O.G.'s doing or part of my new awareness, I stole a mental glimpse of all those thrones, now filled with empty clothes and tubes.

The Redactors were dead, every last one.

"Long live the writers," I whispered and sat up, aware of the agony and also the void of the grey F.O.G., now emptied of the Redactors and their hunger, Now blank, like a fresh page. Now, at long last, *ready.*

I closed my eyes and focused on the memory of the sundial's face, frozen once more one second after time unstuck. We had trapped the Redactors, taken back the energy they stole, but my destiny was not yet complete.

I was Bernadette Bistany's grandson. My situ was the Librarian. I was Bibliopolis, the lost city of books, and I had a special duty.

I channeled all of the stolen energy back from the Redactors into the city contained within my head and declared, "*Bibliopolis…Rise!*"

The ascension passed with a sound like the rustle of pages as a book opened. All of the words poured forth, filling the grey matter of my brain. Every comedy and tragedy, dream, and nightmare. All that was known and recorded and written emerged to fill a different kind of library: the human brain.

I trembled, shook, and transferred the words along my new data port into the F.O.G. and to the souls plugged in, held paralyzed, and dying at the hands of the Redactors. In that glorious moment, I sensed the stories passing into them, cataloguing in the previously dormant storage capacity of their grey matter. The lost history and literature, found once more, filled us.

Download complete.

* * *

Dressed in rags recovered from the cathedral floor, I levitated, moving toward the cell door. One wave of my hand, and the locks released. The door opened. Hunter stood. He motioned with his chin. The ties binding his wrists dropped. He straightened and licked his lips. His wounds instantly healed.

"You did it, Palermo," he said.

"With your help—and the Librarian's."

We rushed together and kissed. I fell into the strength of Hunter's arms, aware of the aura now embossing his skin.

"I love you," he said.

We kissed again. I loved him and the waves of light that were rippling off both of our bodies—and off of all of humanity's evolved members.

The Dark Age of the Redactors was over.

Hands held, we walked out of the cathedral. Around us, people gathered or levitated around the eternal flame in time to watch it die.

The dawn sun inched its way up from the horizon and showed that P.F.R. flags were already down. I knew they would never be raised again. A strange glow filled one corner of still dark sky. Happiness filled me.

"Haley's Comet," I said. "It's returned."

Hunter followed my gaze up to the breathtaking sight. "And now?"

"Now, it's a new time. A time to heal the planet and our hearts. To reconnect the words to the page and never allow this to happen again. It is the first day. It's *once upon a time.*"

"Or *in the beginning*," Hunter said.

"Better yet, *Chapter One*," I said, holding onto Hunter at sunrise on the first enlightened new day in human history.

THE END

ABOUT THE AUTHOR

Raised on a healthy diet of creature double features and classic SF TV, Gregory L. Norris writes regularly for numerous short story anthologies, national magazines, novels, and the occasional episode for TV or film. Gregory novelized the NBC Made-for-TV classic by Gerry Anderson, *The Day After Tomorrow: Into Infinity* (as well as a sequel and a forthcoming third entry into the franchise for Anderson Entertainment in the U.K.), a movie he watched as an eleven-year-old sitting cross-legged on the living room floor of the enchanted cottage where he grew up. Gregory won HM in the 2016 Roswell Awards in Short SF Writing. He once worked as a screenwriter on two episodes of Paramount's Star Trek: Voyager. Kate Mulgrew, Voyager's "Captain Janeway," blurbed his book of short stories and novellas, *The Fierce and Unforgiving Muse,* stating, "In my seven years on Voyager, I don't think I've met a writer more capable of writing such a book—and writing it so beautifully."

In late 2019, Gregory sold an option on his modern Noir feature film screenplay, *Amandine*, to the new Hollywood production company Snarkhunter LLC, owned by actor Dan Lench, a devotee of Gregory's writing. In late 2020, Snarkhunter optioned Gregory's tetralogy Horror film based upon four of his short stories, *Ride Along.* Twice Norris has been nominated for the Pushcart Prize. He is the author of the novel *Ex Marks the Spot* (Woodhall Press) and the forthcoming release of SF tales of wonder and adventure stretching from Sol to Pluto, *The Solar System* (September 2022).

Gregory lives and writes at Xanadu, a century-old house perched on a hill in New Hampshire's North Country with spectacular mountain views, with his rescue cat and emerald-eyed muse. Follow his literary adventures at: www.gregorylnorris.blogspot.com.

Love Books?

Support Authors - buy directly from independent publishers. This puts more royalty dollars into the pockets of your favorite author – and gives them time to write their next book.

Visit us for links to our other books as well as many other vibrant publishing companies to find the book for you.

These ARE The Books You've Been Looking For.

Vanvelzerpress.com